THE MANSION
OF CERVANTES

THE MANSION
OF CERVANTES

CRISTINA L. VAZQUEZ

To Maricela,
So glad we got to
chat and share a mutual love
for the Law as well as storytelling!
I hope you get a few laughs out of this book.
And if you don't, Place the blame on dad!

gatekeeper press™
Columbus, Ohio

THE MANSION OF CERVANTES

Published by **Gatekeeper Press**
2167 Stringtown Rd, Suite 109
Columbus, OH 43123-2989
www.GatekeeperPress.com

Library of Congress Control Number: 2021948748

ISBN (hardcover): 9781662920448
ISBN (paperback): 9781662920455
eISBN: 9781662920462

CONTENTS

PROLOGUE

Austria 1935

From the rearview mirror of the vehicle, I glared silently at the raging flames behind me. The splendor of lights and the imminent destruction of the most beautiful structure I had ever laid eyes on shook me to the core. Snowflakes covered the windows while the tiny clock on the dashboard struck midnight. The swell of tears drowned my eyes and sunk my soul into an avalanche of emotion. Resting in the back seat of the vehicle, I wrapped my arms around my legs in a half-fetal position, feeling the hot stinging sensation of the burns on contact. I screamed. Walking through that fire a thousand times, would have been easy, if it meant seeing him once more. A low groan oozed through my gritted teeth. The car's engine roared to life. The grinding of the gears shifting forward, and the smell of rotten eggs rising from the fumes repulsed me. My gown was soaked with sweat and was cold as ice. I closed my eyes and held my breath. My thoughts swirled aimlessly in my head. I capsized into the back seat of a 1934 Mercedes Benz. It was one of the first vehicles sold in the European market that boasted, among other things, a heating system and air conditioning. The inside revealed two flues inserted on either side of the seat, and a fan circulated air throughout the passenger compartment. Years ago, the experience excited me. Now it meant nothing. I wrapped myself in the grey wool quilt the driver gave me and rubbed my hands. The winters in Austria are cold and unforgiving, but the wonder of the land transcends even the iciest climate.

I arrived in Austria a year ago. The Cervantes family's lawyer invited me to work for the estate as an expert in occult sciences. He employed me to investigate allegations of a haunting at the Mansion of Cervantes. Indeed, I did not meet the family's portrait of an ideal investigator—not by birth and not by wealth. Spanish royalty, with history rich in tradition, frowned upon women like me, of modest means, inexperienced in worldly things, and, worst of all, a seer. I knew the odds were stacked against me. A Spanish newspaper in Malaga in May of 1930 reported the scandalous claims of a trusted seer of the family's matriarch, Mrs. Victoria Alameda De Cervantes. Once the feature became public, the woman disappeared. I feared a similar fate would befall me. Seers were not openly invited to the homes of the rich and famous. They were ostracized for being different. They were freaks, jesters, or just plain crazy. They were kept secret for fear of shame and scandal. What if they told the truth, or worse, they learned the secrets of the wealthy? If they knew my past, they would have certainly ousted me! This family held deadly secrets that would destroy them all if private matters were suddenly unearthed and exposed to the public.

But not all the members of that family were unscrupulous. Some were different, worthy of honor. Who was which? The answer laid hidden within my psyche, as much as it did within the secrets of the east wing of the mansion. The forbidden wing rested on the water's edge, where the legend of a woman's death had marked the Cervantes family forever. A haunting involving past events often swirling around town, like a beast, clasping its claws over its inhabitants. Was that place truly haunted? Or just someone obsessed with conjuring up the past?

The mansion sat on a cliff overlooking the Danube River. A prime location for vacationers, young and old. In the late 1890s, it was known as the pinnacle of social gatherings with many dukes and counts in attendance at the family's annual spring ball. The air surrounding the property was as pure as I had ever breathed. The stunning views of greenery overlooking the landscape in spring took my breath away. The gardens brimming with flowers budding in summer displayed an oasis of red, purple, and pink bouquets. The snow-covered mountains in the winter comforted me and warmed my soul. Even with all that splendor, I spent a year chasing shadows in every corner of the mansion. I struggled with the ability to use my gift as a seer. And often wondered if the powers that be had summoned me there to test my self-confidence and worth.

The seduction of a proper salary and a chance to travel the world drew me in. The stock market crash of 1929 left me reeling and struggling to pay the bills. Despite turning a small profit prior to my journey to Austria, the business lacked stability. The opportunity of earning a similar salary elsewhere was scarce. During the year in Austria, I wondered if my ego demanding to prove itself, had placed me in such peril? Deep down I wanted a challenge and the chance to rise to it. How wrong was I! This would be the most formidable challenge of my life. But I could not deny him! The mystery man haunting my dreams, would be my savior in a world of ghosts, shadows, and the unknown. He guided me through a labyrinth of mystery and chaos. It wasn't clear to me until I arrived at the Mansion on January 20, 1934. His portrait hung on the wall at the entrance of the living room and then I knew! The call to that faraway place was indeed my destiny.

CHAPTER 1

Gifted

On September 15, 1908, my tiny body cascaded out of mother's birth canal—easily. I heard her tell my sister Emma. She gave birth to me at the ripe age of thirty-nine. One of her proudest moments, she boasted. As the head of a staunchly Catholic family, the woman devoted her life to serving God. She set her social affairs to coincide strictly with those of the local church. The inhabitants of the city of Toledo, Spain often consulted with the local priest on issues ranging from spiritual guidance to child rearing and matrimonial counseling. Every child in the home must perform the appropriate sacraments as mandated by the Catholic Church. She demanded.

One evening at the age of six, while I slept soundly, I awoke after feeling the heavy presence of a person breathing down my neck. My sisters Emma and Lillian slept beside me, a custom of most children in the town where I grew up. The strange presence moved slowly down my arms and caressed my skin. It frightened me. The mere thought of an unknown entity launching an assault upon my young body, while I slept, still offends me. Snippets of light peered through the window. My gaze circled the room, searching for the culprit. I heard the pitter-patter of light rain on the windowsill. The firm stroke, moving atop the pale blue duvet that covered me, utterly frightened me. As the youngest of the three, I called on my sisters for help. Emma was the oldest at thirteen. Lilian followed at eleven. The inescapable hands raised the duvet above me, settling on my warm skin. I felt the cold hands and jumped up startled. "Who goes there?" The terror gripped my throat, choking the words out of my mouth. Strands of my short, blonde hair stuck to the sides of my cheeks and soaked in my tears. The curls of my lashes stuck together in clumps. I rubbed my eyes.

"Emma, Lillian, which of one of you touched me?" I stood over the "drunk" girls, asleep and oblivious to my plight. Emma turned away from me muttering,

"Stop, Carolina, let me sleep!" she said, covering her body from head to toe. Silence.

My gaze once again drew me towards the walls and the darkness of the room. A shadow crawled near the window in an upward position like a spider. The black blob-like figure, slithering up and down the walls until it reached the ceiling, left me soaked in my own urine, then disappeared. Its presence lingered around me. My sister's loud snores made me anxious. I wanted to leap out of my bed and run as fast as I could towards my father's room. My rock! My Savior! But I knew my mother would disapprove of such childish behavior, and I would be punished in return, so I patiently bore the dreadful feeling in silence. Ugh.

I covered myself from head to toe and prayed to God and all the saints to save me from that nightmare. One night of terror was followed by many. The daily prayers failed to spare me from the torment of shadow-like figures, soft whispers, and physical attacks. Hair pulling, shoving, kicking, and the piercing shrieks from invisible entities kept me awake most nights. When I managed to sleep through the night, I travelled to other dimensions and met beings from other planets. Most did not frighten me, but their appearances varied: from human form with long torsos to reptile form with short bodies.

The reptilians would show me wars on other planets, explosions, and fire—strange creatures clothed with long, brown tentacles and beady eyes. They sucked the life out of anyone who came near them. The victims' brains often exploded into bloody mush. Some aliens had big, round heads and tiny bodies. They showed me visions of people on white stretchers with wires protruding from every orifice. Large metal contraptions always wrapped around their heads. The wires connected to the metal cap were dipped into jars filled with a translucent liquid, unlike anything I had ever seen on earth. Every time a human awakened; it was always the same reaction. They screamed loudly when they didn't have a tube blocking the airway. I didn't care for it.

The tall, white-skinned humans were the nicest. They were the closest in physical appearance to our species. Those beings were eight- to nine-feet tall. Their slim, white bodies smooth as glass—translucent and often covered in pure white light. Their spines grew longer than earthly humans, like tails between their legs. The long chords extended from their coccyx down to their calves. They spoke telepathically, always calling for peace for our planet. At an early age, I knew that my experiences at nightfall were difficult to endure and hard to explain.

"How did you get that scratch?" Mother asked.

"The ghost from last night!" I replied.

But soon those answers would turn me into a psychopath in my family's eyes. My parents, desperate for answers, called the priest on a regular basis. They begged him to exorcise me, because I was tormented by demons, my mother claimed. But the priest refused time and again.

"Miss Del Valle, your little girl is too young for an exorcism. Besides, she has an active imagination. You must not fret," he would say.

"Pray a novena. That should help your little girl."

Week after week, my mother consulted the priest on the same events, and the prayers were leading nowhere. Toledo, Spain, although small, became my own personal hell. Everyone gossiped. Thank God, the priest refused my mother's pleas. My anecdotes caused him laughter. He thought they were a product an overactive imagination. But to my misfortune, the following years were worse than the nightmare I lived daily with my sisters.

"There goes the crazy Carolina," said Emma. "What demons have you summoned today, psycho?" My eyes filled with tears.

"None! Leave me alone!" I shoved Emma out of the way. But her taunting was endless.

At the age of nine, I travelled to my usual spot by the grocery store, after experiencing the onslaught of criticism hurled at me by Emma. My sister Emma was short-tempered and impulsive when it came to me. She was immediately ready to punch, kick, pull my hair, and throw me across the room when necessary. But that part of her personality, mother seemed to like. However, Emma's stubby figure and short stature exasperated mother, often reminding her that Emma resembled my father. Her pale white skin blotched the minute the sun shone on it while mother often achieved the perfect tan when stepping into the sun. She pestered my sisters incessantly about hiding my father's genetic imprint in public. Since they looked so much alike, they could have been identical twins. But I believed they were beautiful women. Mother valued pin-thin figures. No matter what she ate, she didn't gain a pound. I took after my mother body wise, but she still hated me.

Those Sunday walks through town, watching families smiling at each other, drinking, chatting, and hugging one another felt like an escape from my own reality. The grocer usually offered a lollipop. My pink and white dress, the bow in my hair, and my sparkly white shoes always attracted compliments from his beloved wife, who worked at the store on Sundays, Tuesdays, and Fridays. She wanted a little girl, but as I later learned, she was unable to have children. Venting the day away became my favorite past time. Sucking on a cherry lollipop and talking to myself, while imagining my life in a castle, eased my stress.

Unfortunately, my spot housed a couple of nosy neighbors debating the town's latest scandal. I paced around them. Hands crossed, pursed lips, narrowed eyes. The women cackled and rolled their eyes while entrenched in the latest about my friend's mother. They stood by the steps near the brick building, talking among themselves.

"Mari, have you seen Celia lately?"

The woman shook her head. "I haven't. Her husband Pedro parades himself around town with his mistress Inez Silva."

"Can you fathom it?" she replied, then inhaled a big puff from her cigarette.

"Well, you know, I told her so. All those extra servings at the church outings would take a toll on her figure sooner or later?" Maria rolled her eyes in disgust. "I mean, can you blame Pedro?" she asked.

I dropped my purse and leaned against the brick wall, catty-corner from the two women. I leaned closer forcing them to acknowledge my presence. The more heavyset woman named Olivia glanced at me but didn't stop her chatter. She coughed through half of her long speech and cackled the rest of the way. Like the piercing trill of magpies, these women's high-pitched chatter felt endless.

"There is no excuse for indulging in sweets when your marriage is in trouble!" Maria said in a huff. "If you ask me, she deserved it."

The dark-haired woman held a coin between her fingers. She dumped it into the right pocket of her red shorts. She arched her back and stretched her arms in the air. Her loud yawn awoke the orange cat laying on the steps beneath her feet. She inhaled a deep puff, as if she wanted to suck the life out of the cigarette. Her cheeks sunk while her eyes bulged out of her head.

"Amiga," she laughed, then dropped her cigarette butt onto the concrete. She stepped on it with the sole of her white sandal. "You only speak that way because you're naturally thin."

Her friend retorted, "Well, darling, I work at it. I barely eat. My husband loves it!"

Maria patted her flat stomach, stretching her slim torso upwards. She sucked in a deep breath. "And he wouldn't dare leave me for another woman, even if she were younger!" Maria said sternly.

"Well, never say never! Men are fickle and there's always the next bus coming in five minutes," Olivia retorted, roaring with laughter. She rested her hand on her hip and waved her index finger at a young woman across the street.

The women's chatter reminded me of mother. She often said, "Little girls should not indulge in sweets too often; no one wants a fat girl for a bride." Just like them, she judged everyone. It angered me. I puffed my chest out and hurled myself towards them. My defiant stance startled them. This was not the first time they gossiped. Twice before, Father Armendariz berated them about gossiping on my corner. They knew I ratted them out, but it did not stop them. They eyed me warily and turned away from me.

"Damn it!" I cried.

"Shush, the crazy girl is right behind us," Maria whispered to Olivia, leaning into her shoulder.

"Yes, just saw that little snitch!" replied Olivia, eyeing me closely.

She leaned away from Maria and shoved her fist in my face. Challenge! I parked myself between the women, refusing to let them have at it. Their feeding frenzy would not go down without a fight! Ready. Set. Go. My legs leaped into the air in the women's direction. Strong hands stopped me dead in my tracks. Mr. Leonardo, the grocer's assistant, wrapped his arms around my waist and picked me up forcefully.

"Where are you going young lady?" he mumbled, my feet and arms dangled in mid-air. "Let me go, let me go!" I screamed.

But the women stepped back and waved me off as if they were swatting flies. Their conversation moved onto unimportant details. I growled at them.

"Go on home, young lady before I call your mother!" he said. He set me down, my cotton skirt crumpled and mussed from his dirty hands.

"Jerk!"

The shrill of my screams fell on deaf ears. I ran out of there so fast that my feet barely touched the ground.

"Annette?" I shouted. "Where are you?" I called again, now in a calmer tone. Nothing seemed to slow the flow of tears. "Can anyone find my doll?" I shouted into the kitchen.

Then I crashed into my living room couch exhausted and upset over what happened at the grocery store. Luisa, the youngest of our maids, came out of the kitchen holding the doll in her left hand.

"Is this what you are looking for?" she asked.

"Annette! Annette! I thought I'd lost you."

I kissed the doll on the cheek and thanked the woman. The doll with blonde curly hair and large blue eyes had been there for me every time I got in trouble. Uncle Paulo bought it on one of his trips to Barcelona. He declared the sharp-eyed toy to be a replica of me. But she was so much more. She slept next to me every night. She accompanied me whenever I got in trouble. She even stood next to me. She was my best friend, my refuge while my family repudiated me.

"As little girls go, dolls don't speak, but their silence is golden," my father always said.

It allowed me to divulge my secrets to her, free from judgment. That meant everything. I loved her more than anyone except my father. He often brought me a glass of milk and a slice of cake when someone in the family scolded me. But father changed. I lost him and my doll. I suppose my parents discarded her, just as they did with me.

CHAPTER 2

Telegram

United States 1933.

"Miss Carolina." I heard a man's voice call out while eyeing the coffee stain on my brand-new yellow dress.

"Who is it?" I called out. No one was at the front door. "Ugh, just bought this last week and now look at me."

On the way to the full-length mirror in my office, I grabbed a glass of water and a cotton napkin and dabbed the soaked napkin on my skirt. Before changing my dress, I emptied the remaining water in the sink near my office. My office although modest, was cozy and warm. The walls covered in floral print livened the room. I took another sip of café con leche. The rich strong taste of dark roast espresso, mixed with scalded condensed milk, tasted like heaven to me. Someone's voice grew closer. He had made his way to my office past the front door entrance without knocking. My eyes furrowed and a small crinkle covered my forehead.

"Mr. Williams, to what do I owe this honor?"

"Miss Carolina, sorry to interrupt, but I just ran here from the post office. There is an urgent telegram for you."

As the man approached, his imposing figure and excited expression startled me. I drew back and stepped aside, pulling away from him. When he got close to my Spanish oak credenza, he dropped an envelope on top of it and removed his brown fedora and leather gloves. I leaned into the arm of my sage green velvet couch—old and worn, but stable. We pulled it out of a dumpster nearly three years ago. I swallowed air as if my life depended on it. Although surprises unsettled me, I grabbed the envelope and read a note.

"What is this about?" I asked.

He noticed the bewildered look on my face and spoke: "I don't know, but it's urgent. I need you to accompany me to the post office immediately. They would not release the telegram to me."

I grabbed my gloves, purse, and hat and headed out the door. The road to the small post office located in the center of town felt endless. The last time I received a telegram was more than six months ago, and it came from my mentor Oscar Heston. His bestseller book *Between the Shadows* had sold one hundred thousand copies in its first run. He was also a colleague of the famous mystic Elliott Kayser, who resided in Virginia Beach and was known for delivering complex instructions on surgeries during his meditations. Mr. Kayser had trained as a local pastor and developed an extraordinary gift as a healer through the information he received. I yearned to follow in their footsteps. I longed for a long career as an expert in the occult.

Distracted and worried, I walked rapidly towards the post office. My mother had fallen ill in Spain, and I was dreading bad news. I decided instead to focus on recalling my first interview with Mr. Heston. This always made me happy. His experiments were phenomenal and it prompted me to follow him from Barcelona four years ago. The thump of heavy footsteps trailed me. I spun around to spot the culprit. It was Harry Jones visibly exhausted.

"Miss Carolina, wait for me. You walk very fast!" he shouted. I suddenly recalled my plans for the evening.

"Oh Harry, I cannot attend the Smith's investigation. You will have to use my equipment; can you handle it on your own? Do you think you are ready?"

The man of twenty-two years smiled at me.

"Of course, Chief, I was born for this."

At his young age, he was already quite an expert in apparitions. Although Harry was not physically attractive, he boasted a nice smile and jet-black hair. His almond-shaped eyes, obscured by the frames of his glasses, deemed his appearance unfavorable, but his charming personality often won the prettiest debutantes. Harry's high IQ and manner of speech captivated even the dullest personalities. It was no coincidence that he charmed me into hiring him as my assistant within the first ten minutes of meeting him. His physical attributes, however, showcased the body of a frail young man. He was tall and thin. The neighbors claimed he suffered from a strange syndrome. Indeed, his debilitating disease, which was called rickets, stemmed from his body's inability to absorb calcium and phosphorus. Harry also suffered from gastrointestinal issues. They prevented the absorption of much needed nutrients and contributed to his diagnosis. Despite his frail physique, his mind was extremely sharp.

"Will you accompany me to the post office, Harry?"

"Sure," he said, joyfully.

"I am feeling a little nervous," I countered.

"Why? Is something wrong?" he asked raising an eyebrow.

"Someone sent me a telegram, and it's urgent! What if this telegram brings me bad news?"

Harry frowned, "Maybe it's good news? You won't know until you get there. Grab my arm, I will walk with you. There is nothing to fear."

I was so thankful for Harry, I held onto his arm without a second thought. Harry had caught up to me five blocks away from the post office. In the time he had been my assistant, he transformed my business ideas into a professional setting. Still, I barely understood how important Harry's presence would be in my life. He possessed the risk-taking qualities I lacked. He unapologetically pushed me to openly advertise my business with the townspeople of Virginia Beach.

The business began with a few neighbors regaling us with their stories of apparitions in their homes. They asked us to investigate the problem and find a solution. Our gig consisted of a three-night review, using a portable recording device and a camera to capture the presence of anomalies. Our team consisted of mostly Harry and me, but there were others who helped us. We often researched the obituaries in the area to link the disturbance, hoping to make a connection to the recently departed. Most of the time, humans created the problem by claiming their homes were "haunted," when in fact, the events had a reasonable explanation.

We were lucky to obtain the recording device from a close friend of Oscar Heston, who lived in Germany and had recently defected from the country for political reasons. The artifact resembled a small victrola and contained a disc that generated 78.26 revolutions per minute. Each recording lasted between three to five minutes. The gentleman transported this and other devices from Germany in secret. Believing the world was coming to an end because of Adolf Hitler and his sycophants, the friend left Nazi Germany. He witnessed the early atrocities showing Hitler's true intentions. He said the furthest place he could go would be to America. At that time, we were not prepared for the horror inflicted by Hitler's Reign of Evil. Gunter Muller was accurate when he said Hitler would destroy many with his ideas. But Hitler was not the only one.

Upon arriving at the post office, Mr. Williams, a man in his forties, was already there. I didn't know him well. I wasn't so sure about his interest in rushing back to the post office with me. Harry followed me into the building. Perhaps Mr. Williams waited for the gossip that followed every small town I had ever set foot on. He leaned over the counter, silent and onerous. And yet, his alluring green eyes stunned me. He nodded and tipped his hat to one side as I walked past him.

"I'm here, what news have you for me?"

He signaled the postman with a quick glance and pointed at me. The man behind the calendar handed me a long, white envelope addressed to Miss Carolina Del Valle written in cursive. The telegram came from Fernando Paladino and Associates, Attorneys at Law. #25 Calle De San Bernardino, Madrid, Spain. I raised an eyebrow in complete confusion.

"Mr. Williams, this is not for me," I said bewildered, then handed the telegram back to him.

But Mr. Williams shook his head.

"I don't know any lawyers, much less this one in Madrid," I countered.

"Chief, what if they know you? Why not give it a chance and read the rest?" Harry interrupted.

I gripped the envelope tightly, almost crumbling the entire telegram. "No, no! I am happy here." I shook my head. "Spain is behind me. You know what happened to me there, don't you?"

Harry nodded. But curiosity got the better of him. He eyed me impatiently.

"What if this is good news?" he demanded. "I know I am your assistant, and I don't want to push, but I really think you should read it once and for all," he finished, stepping away from me.

"You're right!" I said, pulling the crumbled piece of paper towards a white table standing on the opposite side of the mailboxes. I smoothed the paper against the top of the table hoping to flatten it.

"Dear Miss Del Valle," I began aloud, "my office represents the Estate of La Familia Cervantes Alameda. My client is an institution in Spain. The Cervantes family has been the subject of every newspaper outlet in Europe as one of the most coveted families since the Reign of King Felipe V."

I adjusted my collar. I caught the eyes of everyone in the post office listening to the contents of the letter as I read it out loud.

"Excuse me," I motioned Harry closer to me.

I whispered, "Harry, please explain, how this is my problem?"

He stared silently, "Chief, if you don't finish the telegram, I can't answer that question." "Ugh," I sighed, "Los Cervantes Alameda have asked me to find an investigator who can travel to Austria and reside with them long enough to solve the mystery."

"Is the Mansion haunted?" Mr. Williams asked, towering over me.

Annoyed, I waived him off and read silently.

"You come highly recommended by Oscar Heston. He said you are experienced and well worth the money. As the Attorney for the Estate, it is my responsibility to place the Mansion for sale once Mrs. Cervantes, the eldest surviving relative passes to a better life. We have attempted to show the mansion to several buyers but the most unfortunate rumor among the townspeople has put a wrench in our plans. They all claim the Mansion of Cervantes is a haunted place. I have been instructed to hire the best person for the job. It pays a salary of thirty-five dollars per week, plus room and board, for as long as you need to stay. There is a ship leaving New York next week. If you are willing to accept the job, you must be on board the *Chaplain* at six o'clock in the morning. This offer expires at midnight on December 16, 1933."

Upon reading the last line, I felt my cheeks flush.

"How dare this stranger give me only twenty-four hours to make such a big decision," I crumbled the letter with such force I would have broken a nail if not for the gloves I wore.

Mr. Williams was staring at me, waiting for an answer, but he would not get one. This was too personal. I thanked him and headed out the door in a hurry. Harry followed behind me in haste.

"Chief, wait for me!" he shouted.

The contents of the letter stunned me—leaving me nervous, hungry, and afraid. Ultimatums often led to disaster in my life. I needed to think. I spotted the bakery one block ahead and launched myself towards it like a high-speed train. I arrived in no time and pushed through front door, disheveled, and famished. The look of confusion on the woman's face behind the counter was startling. Her short, plump frame, red cheeks, and strawberry-blonde hair barreled toward me.

"May I help you, Miss Del Valle? Are you well?" she asked.

"Ah, yes Mrs. Wentworth, forgive my intrusion. I was afraid I was too late to collect the chocolate cake and cookies I ordered yesterday."

I tried to calm myself. Spectacles were unwelcomed, and I did not need any more gossip coming my way.

"Oh sure Miss Del Valle, I almost forgot. Wait here."

The woman left, and I heard the bell ring behind me. The flash of my reflection in the mirror behind the counter caught my attention. My curls covered my pale face. The beads of sweat plastered on my forehead left me embarrassed. I pulled out my Guilloche loose powder compact my friend Leticia gave me before leaving Spain. I powdered my cheeks, forehead, chin, and nose.

Someone opened the door. "Chief, he whispered, what's going on? Did I miss something?" Harry took a deep breath, exhausted.

Poor Harry—always chasing after me. He spotted a table with two chairs and dropped like a sack of potatoes. His torso slumped over the arm of a chair taking a brief rest until he heard Mrs. Wentworth's footsteps heading back from the café area. The old woman had recently installed a commercial espresso machine just like the one she saw in New York City.

"Good evening, Mr. Jones, can I get you anything?" Harry nodded. "Double espresso please!"

She turned to me.

"Make that two, thank you."

Harry held his hand out to me, and I handed him the crumpled paper. He read the telegram.

He eyed me and smiled. "This is our first big job. We must be on that ship next week," he said, taking a sip of his coffee.

"Harry, what are you talking about? I still don't know if I want to go, and if they would let you come along." Harry's shoulders sank. He took another sip.

"Oh Harry, no. I can't," I shook my head vigorously. I grabbed my cup and swallowed quickly, burning my throat in the process. I flinched. "We know nothing about that family. We don't even speak the language."

"They are Spanish, like you. Of course, they speak our language," Harry smiled wryly.

He always managed to talk me into risky alternatives when it came to investigations, but this was a walk on the wild side and too far. Nevertheless, Harry and I had become a business enterprise. Partners in crime. Family. Besides, the pay was extraordinary. It didn't take much for me to accept. I would only travel abroad if Harry was allowed to accompany me. Those would be my terms. If they did not agree, there would be no trip.

Surprisingly, Mr. Paladino immediately approved Harry's travel without a salary, but I would share mine with him. We departed from the Statue of Liberty in New York on December 20, 1933. A snowstorm of more than ten inches covered the city in blankets of snow. The freezing cold left us shivering at the crack of dawn. Luckily, we made the ship in time. It would take approximately thirty days to reach our destination. The itinerary estimated the ship to cross the Atlantic in two weeks' time. Thereafter, a trip from London to Paris via a small plane was the next part of the trip. A stop in Madrid for a briefing with Mr. Paladino followed. Finally, our journey concluded by train from Paris to Vienna where a driver of Mrs. Alameda De Cervantes delivered us to the mansion. We had planned for a month's stay.

CHAPTER 3

The Voyage

We boarded the majestic ocean liner, excited by the great adventure awaiting on the other side of the Atlantic. The transatlantic ship, dubbed the *Chaplain*, made its debut June 1, 1932, with its exclusive route from the port of London along the River Thames to the North Sea. Thereafter, it traveled directly to the port of the Statute of Liberty in the United States of America. Other passenger ships travelled at a slower pace, but the superliners traveling the North Atlantic between Europe and North America, boasting larger passenger capacity, moved faster. The *Chaplain* made the trip across the Atlantic in fifteen days. Others took a month to reach London. The *Chaplain* was one of the largest, fastest, and most luxurious ships at sea—a ship of dreams. Some people compared it to the *Titanic*, but any resemblance to the *Titanic* and its demise only troubled me. Tragedy stalked me. This trip, I hoped, would be different. Marvelous. Maybe.

The sun peeked through the horizon upon arrival at the dock. We waited in line while I rummaged through my purse looking for my passport.

"Chief, don't forget our tickets and the itinerary Mr. Paladino sent you," Harry said shaking.

"Got them right here!"

I pointed to the large, thick envelope. My cheeks were so red from the cold, I wrapped half of my face between two scarves. As we passed through customs, Harry spotted a young man handling our luggage. His excitement was palpable.

"This ship is amazing," Harry said. "On my salary, this trip appeared impossible."

"Yes, I already know, we are funded by a very wealthy family. What I still don't understand is why Mr. Heston recommended me for this job? He is so famous. Any of his colleagues would have been just as apt to perform this investigation."

Harry pulled a long cigar out of his suit pocket and lit it. He raised his hand, pointing his finger in the air.

"About that, Chief," he continued, "this may be linked to Gunther Muller, the Germans, and our equipment."

"Mr. Muller is involved in this?" I inquired.

He nodded while watching a young man loading our luggage.

"Watch it! That equipment is very rare."

The man placed the box slowly and deliberately on the floor. "Sorry, Sir, I didn't realize." Harry shoved his hands in the air towards the man.

"It's okay, this is a special recorder. You can't throw this around like the rest of the luggage," Harry said with a grimace.

"May I ask what that recorder is for," he said.

"I would tell you but it's a secret mission," Harry retorted.

I rolled my eyes at him, "It's too early for secret missions, don't you think?"

Harry dropped his head with a grin. "You are right, Chief."

That evening we dined in the ballroom. They served pheasant breasts a l'orange with dried apricots. They served roasted potatoes and baked green beans. The waiters refilled our champagne flutes several times over. Some patrons indulged all night. After three glasses of the bubbly, my head started spinning. People's fascination with champagne never ceased to amaze me. The sour taste of alcohol followed by a flushed face, slurred speech, and slow movements left me feeling out of control. My dulled senses and the pounding headache that usually followed outweighed any desire to drink excessively. Yet, there I was, struggling to rise from my table, holding onto the chairs for balance—the room full of strangers talking and laughing. There were the women sharing anecdotes about their next trip to Paris for Chanel's spring collection. Harry and I, the outsiders, had inadvertently pierced the special cult of society called the "rich." We sat among them, but we were nothing like them.

Harry excused himself to visit the restroom while I sat trapped next to a heavyset woman with a large red hat. She blocked my view of the stage. Every time she turned her head, her hat's white feathers brushed against the side of my face. As much as I detested sitting there, it made me laugh. A comical twist in my journey to Austria. The grandeur of the *Chaplain* would never be forgotten. Long golden drapes hung from floor to ceiling in the ballroom. Ornaments of gold dressed the balcony in the dining room. White porcelain vases in every corner filled with vibrant and colorful blends of delphiniums, lilies of the valley, tulips, asters, and chrysanthemums. A red velvet carpet was draped over the marble stairs. The ornate balustrades of gold and silver lent an air of elegance. The costly style reflected similar designs found in many European magazines.

Although I felt we were the only outliers, droves of passengers looked around the ballroom with their mouths wide open as if they had never seen such opulence aboard an ocean liner before either. The stuffiness of the place dulled my senses causing me to push through the double doors and run towards the bow of the ship. The cold air burned my cheeks. The chill froze me, but I did not care.

A random image had materialized in my mind. It reminded me of someone I knew long ago. Who was he? What did he want? The stranger in my dreams! If only a figment of my imagination? Ever since we boarded the ship, a sudden angst had rippled through me. His face, his lips! An unknown portrait, lingering somewhere in time. Going nowhere. I inhaled deeply, centering myself into nothingness. The chill in the air, amid the silent night, felt glorious. A slow rhythmic sound of the waves, while the boat bobbed back and forth, eased my pounding headache.

"Carolina Del Valle, is that you?" said a strange voice. I spun around trying to locate the source. When I saw him, I wanted to die!

"Ivan, what are you doing here?

"Well, sis, I could ask the same of you?" He took off his coat and handed it to me.

"No thank you, I'm fine!" I replied.

"Carolina, please, I come in peace, really. Take my coat, you're freezing."

I nodded and he walked towards me and gently placed the coat over my shoulders.

The blond man with the pale blue eyes stood there, calculating his next move. He took a puff from his pipe and sighed, "So, where were we?"

I barely looked at him. I stared directly at the calm waves while he spoke.

"So, are you here with a man?"

"I don't owe you any explanations," I countered.

"Oh so, I am your brother, and you are galivanting with a man on this boat! And you don't think you owe me an explanation!" He glared at me.

I removed his coat and handed it back to him.

"Half-brother. And I owe you nothing!" I said furiously.

"You can't deny it; I saw you with him! And you are his lover."

The blood rush warmed my skin. I raised my hand and felt the swift slap of my hand strike his cheek. Then I stepped back, shocked at my own boldness.

CRISTINA L. VAZQUEZ

"How dare you?" I reproached.

Ivan grabbed me by the arm with one hand and pulled my skirt with the other. He ripped my skirt apart with just one pull. Then he shoved me towards the stairwell, leading up to the captain's quarters. His face flushed with rage, ready to pounce on me.

"I see that you're the same stubborn child I remember. Does he know?" I tried to shake his grip, but he was too strong.

"Does he know what?" I demanded.

"Does he know about your past?" he challenged.

"Ivan, release me this minute! I don't know what you're talking about," I pleaded.

The sound of footsteps grew near us.

"Let's go. Someone's coming, and I don't want to cause a scene!" he said in a low voice. I kicked him in the shin, and he let me go.

"Angry with your brother, are you?" he smiled.

I glared at him. I buried my face in a handkerchief, trying to wipe away my tears.

"Miss Carolina," Harry shouted as he approached with the ship's security officers. "Are you all right?" he asked.

I was shaking uncontrollably.

"Chief, did he hurt you?" He stared at my wrinkled dress and disheveled curls.

"Officers, no need for alarm, I assure you. My sister is just cold, and we had ourselves a little family reunion tonight. Isn't that right, Carolina?" He glared at me nervously.

I stammered my words, "Yes, yes, that is correct!"

Harry's clenched jaw, intense glare, and furrowed brows frightened me.

"So, we are done here?" Ivan asked.

"Not so fast, sir, you have obviously frightened Miss Del Valle." Harry stared him down.

. 31 .

One of the officers intervened, "Now gentlemen, there is no need to escalate the situation."

The officer leaned in towards Ivan and whispered, "Sir? I think it's best if you accompany me away from this scene, right now!" Ivan agreed.

The man directed my brother away from me.

"After you!" he said. I watched Ivan being escorted out of the area and back to the dining room where the redheaded woman greeted us. I stared at him silently. Harry, still angry, paced back and forth.

"Chief? What was that all about? Did he hurt you?"

I shook my head. Before he spoke again, I raised my hand to silence him.

"Let's get out of here and I will tell you all about it!"

Harry followed me out of the area, keeping a close eye on Ivan. Harry's counterpart matched his death stares. This would be war! Ivan would not stop until he found me again. He had spewed utter disdain for Harry and eventually this would become a problem.

That evening, I sobbed in my room, recounting my dreadful history with Ivan. A child of infidelity, he blamed his sins on my father's abandonment. My father frequented a brothel in town and women threw themselves at him. One evening, he met a woman named Eva Duarte. She became his lover and soon Ivan was born. When mother learned of the infidelity, she forced my father to join the church. She forbade us from having any contact with Ivan or his siblings. She prevented Ivan from sharing our last name. As a child, he beat cats and dogs and lit them on fire. He stole food and cash from anyone he could, including the blind. He preyed on the weak and the homeless, children and women. When he turned twelve, he begged the priest to let him be an altar server. His only intention was to steal donations. The priest had unwillingly given in. Ivan stole donation money every Sunday until he turned eighteen. After that, he stole from widows. Whenever he saw me or my sisters at church, he kicked, slapped, and stole from us.

"Whatever he is doing here, it is not good. He is dangerous!" I finished.

Harry eyed me quizzically. "Your brother is not rich then?" he asked.

"No, I don't think so!" I replied. "He must be scamming someone here out of a fortune. Maybe the ginger?"

Harry curled his moustache. "Chief, we can help her and then ensure he never finds us again!"

I stood up from my chair, aggravated. "No. We need to avoid him at all costs, Harry! If he is taking advantage of that woman, we must not interfere!"

Harry eyed me. "That is not who you are!" He paced around the room awkwardly.

He served himself a glass of brandy on the rocks from the bar in my suite.

"We have to save her from that monster!" he insisted.

Over the next two weeks we managed to plot our every move. We avoided him as much as we could. He was busy asking questions about us, but no one knew anything! The night before our arrival in London, we dined in the ballroom. We expected Ivan to approach us, and we took advantage of the time to warn his partner of his evil ways.

"Miss Del Valle, it is so nice to see you again!" Ivan said, holding a glass with cognac in his hand.

I was sipping my chicken soup when I noticed him. A tall, slim, redheaded woman stood beside him. He smiled at me, then gently, approached me. The woman, dressed in a green satin dress, clung to his arm. The sight of him numbed me. I nodded in his direction and continued.

Harry, dressed in a black tuxedo one size too big, approached the table. "Ah Mr. Duarte, such a pleasure to see you again."

The man smiled, "Of course, Harry, is it?" Harry nodded. "Sister, you must meet my wife Ginger Stevens!" Ivan said in a high-pitched voice. The woman's face appeared disgruntled.

"Sister?" she answered, then nudged my brother. "You don't have any sisters, Ivan. I would know!"

I rose from my chair and extended my hand to her.

"Half-sister, Ms. Stevens. It's a pleasure to meet you; I am Carolina Del Valle."

Ivan winced. "Darling, my sister and I haven't seen each other since, you know, that unfortunate incident when she was fifteen years old."

The woman placed her hand on her bosom.

"Oh, darling, that's her! You never told me she was your sister! I always pictured the person to be a distant relative."

She eyed me from head to toe.

"Oh darling, come here you need a hug!"

She stretched her arms out to me. Before I knew it, she was already there, wrapping herself around my torso. Her scent was so strong that I almost choked. I smiled nervously.

"Ms. Stevens, I am not sure what Ivan has told you about me, but I assure you, I am fine. In fact, I am on a work trip. This is my assistant Harry Jones," I said curtly.

She smiled at me, "Oh, well, I am so glad to hear that. Why don't you both join us for a nightcap later?"

I glanced at Harry. He nodded. We arranged to convene at the Luxemburg's Lounge on Deck 5 at 10:00 p.m. We never showed. We snuck into their bedroom with the help of our friend Reese and left a note for Ginger in her jewelry box. The next day we departed, hoping to never see him again. We were wrong!

CHAPTER 4

Abandoned

"DEATH," I exhaled in a faint whisper. The impact of that strange word coupled with the vision of Martin's vehicle veering sharply into an embankment made my knees buckle. His handshake overwhelmed me.

"Quick. Everyone, help! Your sister fainted!" my father shouted. "Did you not hear me? The child has fainted! Someone, call the doctor and help me pick her up!"

In those days, he became easily agitated. A product of his guilty conscience. He feared God's wrath in losing one of us. He did not realize his infidelity would be the least of his sinful transgressions. My father paid a significant price for the choices he made, especially with his own children.

"My dear Caro, please wake up!" he said trembling. When I did not respond, he slapped me on the face repeatedly. "Wake up, daughter, I don't want to lose you." His forceful assault on me did more harm than good. I knew he meant well, but his handprint marked my face for several hours. My eyes fluttered.

"Oh, sweet child!" he muttered. "I thought we lost you for a moment. Are you well?" he whispered. I opened my eyes, flustered by the commotion. My sister Emma appeared hysterical, as usual, whenever I said or did anything to offend her. Her eyes swimming in a sea of tears. She wore a pink rose pinned onto the bosom of her matching dress. The rose lay lobsided, bobbing up and down every time she threw her hands up in the air. It was hard for me to take her seriously.

I gazed at Martin, her betrothed. The nicest man in the universe as far as it concerned me. He loved my sister and wanted to marry her. That's all I cared about. Martin's bewildered eyes darted around the room as everyone spoke their piece. When it came to me, he just stared. I almost fainted again. My sister held onto Martin's hand so tightly, squeezed his hand visibly and showing the white of his knuckles. Her defiant stance and finger-pointing went overboard. Maybe it was part show for Martin's sake or maybe it was fear that it might be true.

"See father, there is nothing wrong with your precious daughter, Caro. She is just fine. I, on the other hand, am insulted and embarrassed once again by her theatrics." She released Martin's hand and paced around the room frothing at the mouth and sobbing uncontrollably. "On his first visit to our home, this is the welcome he gets."

She glared at me furiously. If allowed, she'd lodge daggers into my heart, but in the presence of our neighbors, she relented. After all, it was a party. My sweet fifteenth birthday. What would the townsfolk think of her? Emma delighted in appearances, and today she would not disappoint the guests. My sister Lillian was just as disgusted as Emma was with me. She could not help but glare at me. Her mouth soured at the mention of my name. In her defense, she was more discreet than Emma. But I never understood why.

"Ladies and gentlemen, please enjoy the festivities," my father said. "Doctor Vazquez is on his way, and I am sure our daughter's fainting spell occurred because she skipped breakfast."

He motioned to Emma and pointed at her and Lillian to follow him to his study. I heard the jangled sounds of my father's navy-blue drapes printed with pink and red roses close. Lillian's clumsy hands clanked father's glasses while she poured wine from the crystal decanter. Behind closed doors, my father attempted to reprimand my sisters for their behavior in public.

"Your insolence has undermined my authority!" he shouted, staring at Emma. He puffed his chest out and lifted his hands shaking them furiously in the air. "I will not tolerate any more insults directed at any member of this family; do you hear me?" The thunderous shouting resonating from my father's study was deafening.

"Father, do you not see that for Carolina, this is the role of the century! She needs an audience and craves attention at my fiancé's expense!" Emma said exhausted. "I just wanted to celebrate my engagement tonight, and she had to ruin it with her crazy antics. How am I supposed to feel?" she asked.

My father lowered his gaze. His strained smile and stooped posture revealed an attitude of surrender in front of Emma. Defeated, he reached out to her in a half-hearted embrace.

"My sweet Emma, please forgive Carolina. You are kind and quite wonderful. I am so sorry this happened, but I assure you, Caro means you no harm. She cannot help it, child." Emma pulled away from him. "Lillian, can you please ask your sister not to walk away from her poor old father?" I heard him say. Lillian's raised cheeks and pulled upper lip gave my father no comfort. She wrinkled her nose in his direction and turned to Emma.

"Come on sister, let's get back to the party. Besides, you don't want other single ladies consorting with your man, do you?" Lillian's comments must have struck a chord with her because I saw them quickly scoot out of my father's study and into the courtyard where the guests were dining.

The doctor tended to me for a few minutes. My father burst through the doors, barely glancing at him. His watery eyes focused in my direction. His bald head, which was bright red, matched his flushed cheeks. Our eyes met momentarily. I lowered my gaze shaking.

"She should be fine. Her sugar dropped and she just needs some cake. No need to worry," the doctor said smiling. He winked at me and then walked over to my father, who was sitting on my bed staring off into the distance.

"Juan Antonio, are you all right?" he inquired. My father barely moved and did not answer his inquiry. Dr. Vazquez asked again, but when my father failed to answer, he narrowed his gaze and puckered his lips.

"Doctor, are you finished?" I asked.

"Yes," he said curtly. He packed his bag and left the room.

In the courtyard, Emma had joined her betrothed. Martin Valdez, dubbed by his friends as the crème de la crème when it came to suitors. He earned a medical degree and planned on establishing his own medical practice in Barcelona. Most of the single young men in Toledo enlisted in the army. The three bachelors, including Martin, had studied for careers. Eduardo Lopez earned a juris doctorate and proposed to Emma's friend, Lydia Valencia. The second bachelor Samuel Vargas graduated as an architect from the University of Madrid. Everyone hoped to match Emma first, so that he would take over father's firm, but he met Anita Torres instead.

Martin became my sister's last hope at a suitable match. At twenty-two years old, most of the townspeople called her an old maid. Martin and Emma fell madly in love. My sister planned to relocate after the wedding. The short and handsome man stood by the wine bar, surrounded by single ladies. He leaned against a stool when Emma pushed her way through the crowd.

"Martin, my love, what's the matter?" Emma inquired. "You look spooked. Are you all right?" The blue-eyed man's forehead appeared drenched in sweat. He shifted his weight uncomfortably, then pulled a handkerchief and wiped his brow.

"What did your sister mean by *death*? Does she mean, I am going to die soon? Is that why you were so upset?" he asked warily.

Emma trembled nervously. "Oh that! No, my love, that is just my crazy sister Carolina. She always wants attention. Please don't fret over her comments."

She grabbed his hand and pulled him towards the dance floor. I watched my sister dance the night away with the love of her life. It made me happy for her, but I knew her happiness was short lived. And I would be blamed for that tragedy just like the rest of the calamities that would eventually befall our family.

That night my mother punished my outburst in the cruelest way. She waited until the last guest left and then locked me in the guestroom away from my sisters. She knew of my nightmares and my fear of sleeping alone, but she didn't care. My so-called visions sickened her. My frequent outbursts overwhelmed her simple-minded theories. She starved me and locked me up. She hid me away from the neighbors. Once a day, she allotted me a piece of bread and a glass of water. She called it "penance" for my sins. I prayed the rosary daily while battling nightly demons in a dark room.

People often spoke of prison. Their ongoing gossip resulted in wrongfully jailing people in town. Yet, I was innocent of any crime, and my sentence was solitude. A prison-like environment, where no one cared whether I lived or died.

Mother lifted my punishment after two weeks. However, my reprieve was short-lived. A week later, my sister received the dreadful news of Martin's passing. Emma's future had disappeared, and she held me responsible. I vividly remember that afternoon when she managed to find me in the courtyard playing with my doll and released her fury upon my frail, fifteen-year-old body. After eating very little for two weeks, I could not resist the forceful beating of my sister. She yanked my hair with such fury, and she kept the clumps to prove it. She punched and kicked me so hard that my lips bled profusely, and my right eye turned black and blue for weeks.

"I'm going to kill you!" she yelled. She lunged at my blue and white polka dot dress and ripped the collar with such force, my buttons spilled all over the concrete floor. The scratches on my neck from Emma's long fingernails ripping through my skin hurt.

"No, Emma, don't!" I screamed, but my sister was livid.

"You killed him! I hate you; you are not my sister."

I tried to run away from her, but she caught me by the arm and lunged at me once more; I grabbed a rock nearby and struck her in the face, leaving a gash of blood. My mother ran over to stop us from fighting, but as usual, I was the bad one. She saw my sister's face gushing with blood and lost it!

"My God, Child, what possessed you to do this?" she demanded. My mother's deadly stare was too much for me to bear, and I cried uncontrollably.

"She tried to kill me; I was just defending myself!" I yelled, but my cries fell on deaf ears.

My sister turned toward mother and sobbed, "Mother, she has ruined me!"

Mother embraced her with compassion. Emma then touched her face briefly and caught a glimpse of her hand drenched in her own blood. She became irate again. She tried to attack me once more, but this time my father intervened.

"Enough is enough, Emma. You're going to kill her!" father said.

"You know what? I want to die, Papa! Your beloved daughter murdered my boyfriend with her witchcraft," Emma said. "Didn't she cause this misfortune? What are they going to say about us? Everyone who comes near us will say she is a witch, or worse, a demon! We will be the talk of the town! Your business is drowning in debt, and I will never find a suitable man!"

Lillian jumped in. "Papa, Emma is right! If you don't handle the situation, it will escalate. I have a life too. What if she does this to one of my friends? Carolina is a witch. She killed Martin with her witchcraft."

My father, dismayed about the situation, sank into the velvet couch in the courtyard; he held his head between his legs. He let out a long sigh and covered his mouth with his fists. My mother and sisters were convinced of the family's continued embarrassment because of me. But even worse, my prediction of Martin's death they deemed it as a curse—one that placed everyone in danger.

After Martin's wake, our home became hell on earth. My best friend Leticia De Alcantara tried her best to sneak into my room and entertain me. Sometimes she played with me. Other times, she brought me cookies and sang songs. Her voice surpassed anyone else's at church in beauty and perfection. High pitched, yet hypnotic, like the sound of an angel. Anything to pass the time in the hell I was living. I swore my mother planned to annihilate me slowly. I felt alone and abandoned by my only ally—my father. His spirits seemed broken as he would spend most days alone in his study when he was not working in town.

As a wealthy architect, he had experienced the highs and lows of the business. Recently, he had lost some projects because of Martin's death. Concerned about the townsfolk, and the declining contracts, he set up a meeting with the local priest, a psychiatrist, Dr. Vazquez, and the entire family.

"We have to fix this problem with Carolina," he spoke. Everyone sat around like the knights of the roundtable, drinking coffee, and opining about my future. They all made suggestions, but no one asked me.

"So, we all agree," Dr. Vazquez said, "the girl needs psychiatric help. We cannot help her. Her visions frighten everyone."

The priest, worried by the suggestion, tried to intervene. "Sons, let's not be impulsive. Carolina is a still girl. To suggest a crazy hospital at that age would be devastating for her."

My mother rose from her chair and raised her hand. "Excuse me, Father Armendariz, this is a family matter. I did not object to this meeting, but I must remind you that Carolina is my daughter, and she needs the care of a hospital."

"But Angela, is it possible that we have reached such extremes?" I heard my father say. "There is no other way?" he asked nervously.

"I am afraid not!" my mother retorted. "I will have the last word as she is my daughter." She stared everyone down, indignant that anyone would question her motives.

"Then, there is nothing more to do," my father said, frowning.

"Not as far as I am concerned," my mother replied. "Given that I have been the only faithful one in this marriage, I am entitled to decide without your input."

My mother rose from the table and asked everyone to leave politely. She turned to my father and my sisters and spoke, "Carolina will depart for the mental hospital in Malaga first thing tomorrow morning."

CHAPTER 5

Austria

In 1918, Vienna, the capital of Austria, strengthened into a reduced, landlocked, central European country that emerged from World War I as a republic. During Hitler's invasion, they dubbed it the "Greater" Vienna, reflecting the Nazi's revision of the city limits. Our journey via train proved to be my favorite leg of the trip. The first-class accommodations and attention to detail provided by every attendant exceeded our expectations.

We disembarked from Vienna at Stadt Bahn, where a young man in his mid-thirties greeted us. The man, with a slim build and brown wavy hair, paced sideways. He stood by the edge of the railroad with a smoke pipe protruding from the side of his mouth and a square, black, and white sign extending from his hands. The sign read: "Carolina Del Valle and Associate. Welcome to Vienna." I immediately spotted the sign with the bold letters. The man waved as the train passed him and finally came to a full stop. We gathered our luggage and stepped off the train. As we approached him, he dropped the sign and marched towards us. His left hand dug into the pocket of his brown vest. I noticed his dark moustache and wide grin.

"Good morning, you must be Carolina Del Valle and, the gentleman, is he your associate?" he asked, gazing at us. "My name is Gaspar Torres Avellanos. I am the chauffeur for the Cervantes Estate."

He smiled crookedly, extending his hand out to me. Harry paused stoically next to me for a few seconds, studying Gaspar. He leaned into me sideways and whispered, "Nervous little guy, isn't he?" I smiled and rolled my eyes.

"You are a native of Spain, correct?" Harry inquired. "I assumed the family would have hired the services of locals."

Gaspar looked up at me and scoffed. He grabbed the last piece of luggage with both hands and shoved it into the vehicle's trunk. He slammed the door shut.

"Of course, the maids are Austrians, but the family prefers to employ Spaniards as well. Most of the Austrian servants have learned to speak Spanish and vice versa," he said, motioning us to follow him towards the vehicle.

"Mr. Torres, I'm Harry Jones, the associate," Harry offered. Gaspar nodded in Harry's direction. Harry crouched down, attempting to help the driver carry the heavy equipment, but his hands slipped. "Oh, I am sorry, sir," Harry spoke, his voice trembling. The driver turned towards him and caught the box just in time. He shoved the luggage in the vehicle's trunk and opened the rear door.

"Señorita Del Valle, after you!" he said, gesturing for me to take a seat. "Mr. Jones, you're American right?"

Harry nodded and smiled. Harry removed his hat and placed it on the front seat. His hands grabbed onto a lever on the right side and adjusted the seat backwards into a reclined position.

"I learned Spanish from my neighbor whose family lived in Puebla, Mexico. My parents encouraged me to spend three summers in Puebla once I turned twelve," Harry offered eagerly.

Gaspar rolled his eyes and walked around the vehicle to the driver's seat.

"We will be there in approximately two hours," he said, as we settled into the passenger seat. Mr. Paladino had warned us about Gaspar. His knack for telling stories about the Mansion even when no one seemed interested was infamous. But I disagreed with Mr. Paladino's assertion. The driver struck me as a genuine individual.

"Señorita Carolina, the Mansion of Cervantes is beyond exceptional," Torres offered. "There is nothing like it around here."

Harry sat beside him on the front seat passenger side of the vehicle, avoiding the awkward stares with the driver but giving him the ability to listen to Gaspar intently.

"Mr. Torres," he said while lighting the man's cigarette. Gaspar frowned. He grabbed the steering wheel with both hands, stretching and twisting, finally settling on an upright position. His eyes rested forward toward the road ahead.

"Well?" Harry asked, leaning forward and taking a puff of his cigarette.

Gaspar remained silent. My torso rested comfortably in the back seat of the vehicle. I closed my eyes and pretended to sleep while Harry probed the chauffer for details on rumors.

"Gaspar, do you smoke?" Harry asked. "Would you like a cigarette?"

Gaspar smiled and nodded. Harry handed him a cigarette, leaned sideways, and lit it. "Thank you," Gaspar replied.

The driver smiled. He dropped one hand from the steering wheel and leaned back into his seat. He took a deep breath and sighed.

"Well, Mr. Jones, since you have been so kind to me, I think it's fair that I return the favor," he said, eyeing the road while he spoke.

"You two are the third set of investigators arriving at the Mansion in the last year since the rumors began."

"What do you mean, Sir?" Harry raised an eyebrow.

My ears perked up, but I pretended to be asleep. I slid my body sideways.

"What happened to the first two sets?" Harry inquired.

"Ah well, a well-known investigator, a man by the name of Johnathan Jenson, led the first group. Former Lieutenant in the U.S. Army even held a Medal of Honor. He fancied himself to be a cross between Sherlock Holmes and Auguste Dupin." Torres roared with laughter. "Mr. Jenson and his comrades seemed too good to be true. They did nothing more than survey the land and drink tea."

"So, they never investigated?" Harry asked.

"Sure, they asked a few questions about the alleged haunting, but nothing came of it. The qualifications they possessed seemed unclear; but upon their arrival at the Mansion, they received the royal treatment. Everyone bowed their heads in unison before those gentlemen. One month into the investigation, they disappeared without a trace. They each received $50 per week plus room and board to investigate. For what? They took the money and ran. No one ever heard from them again."

Harry sat up. "Mr. Torres, you mean they just disappeared? No, note. No goodbye?" Harry protested.

Gaspar took another puff of his cigarette.

"Yes sir, that's right," he responded.

I sat up. "Gaspar, what about the police? Did anyone alert the police about their disappearance?" I protested.

"No. Mrs. Alameda De Cervantes refused to alert the authorities, claiming Mr. Jenson sent her a letter two months later apologizing for his abrupt departure. I don't buy it," Gaspar declared.

His conviction blew me away. My eyes widened and my mouth dropped open. Gaspar eyed me from his rearview mirror and made a comment.

"Señorita Del Valle, sounds like no one warned you about the family," he scoffed.

I shook my head.

"I know nothing of them and now I am worried. What are we walking into?" I said nervously.

Harry pulled his moustache down calmly. He turned to the driver and asked, "Which one is she?"

"You mean Mrs. Eugenia Arguelles De Cervantes?" Gaspar countered.

He positioned his rearview mirror directly in front of me. He raised one eyebrow and spoke. Harry nodded.

"She is the widow of Captain Esteban Arturo Cervantes Alameda. They share a daughter named Natalia Beatriz Cervantes Arguelles, heir to the estate, along with the elder Mrs. Alameda De Cervantes and her daughter Jacqueline. Captain Esteban died ten years ago in this mansion of an unknown cause, and his sister Jackie left the mansion after his death, vowing to never return."

Harry frowned. He took another puff of his cigarette and smashed the butt into the ashtray.

"The whispers in town claim Señor Esteban's widow planned his death, and that she paid a foreign doctor to sign the death certificate. But no one has ever seen the death certificate. Rumor has it she paid off every officer in this town to avoid exhuming the body for testing."

Harry immediately protested. "Sir, be careful with your accusations! That is very serious, and you can lose your job!" His serious face, coupled with his tense stance and arms lying flat across his chest, made me anxious.

"Mr. Jones, forgive me, but you strike me as a serious gentleman. It behooves me to warn you against the perils of falling prey to Mrs. Arguelles De Cervantes and her sidekick Josef the butler. No one knows his last name or where he came from, but he is the widow's right hand. They are merciless!"

Harry's cheeks flushed. "I am not sure what you mean by that. Are you suggesting murder?" Harry retorted.

The word murder scared me. I threw my body into the center console and shook Harry's arm, motioning him to stop the questions—but it was too late for that. Gaspar continued regaling us with the town's conspiracy theories about the Cervantes family. It turned my stomach. I wasn't sure whether to be sick or lie down and feign ignorance. He lowered the window and blew smoke into the air. When Gaspar felt the cold breeze fill the interior of the vehicle, he rolled the window up halfway.

"As I was saying, things at the mansion are not what they seem. Be careful who you trust. Better yet, trust no one! Except the cook Mrs. Frances and yours truly!" he demanded.

"What happened to the second set of investigators?" Harry asked.

"Ah, Mr. Giannini Ven gales, former Captain of the Naval Guard in Roma, Italia. Sad to say, he drowned in the river two weeks after he arrived. I had faith in his investigation as he had claimed that someone was tampering with the mansion's lighting devices, and he believed the haunting was a hoax. I heard him mention it to his colleague Bardolino Benigni Magnotta one evening while I drove them to town for a couple of beers. They spoke Italian, but Spanish is close enough. I understood every word he spoke. He feared something far more sinister than a haunting was afoot. Mr. Magnotta disagreed. The next morning Senor Magnotta departed early, deeply disturbed by what he witnessed. He was so afraid that he sent a letter to Mr. Paladino with his concerns. Mr. Ven Gales, however, described his investigation as peculiar, but he declared the haunting claim to be unfounded. I suppose his letter to Mr. Paladino prompted your arrival," Gaspar explained.

"Who is the Cervantes family then? Why have they summoned us here?" I asked Gaspar.

"Señorita Del Valle, I am not sure why you are here. You are both young compared to your predecessors. No offense, but I thought this was a joke when I saw you both arrive at the station."

I bit my lip, trying to calm my nerves. "Gaspar, can we trust you?" I asked.

Gaspar pulled over, turned the engine off, and spun around to face me.

"Certainly!" he spoke. "I am not sure what qualifications you have for these sorts of investigations, but it is clear you have good contacts. Mr. Paladino would not divulge this information to just anyone. Someone must exalt you!" he said.

"Why are you so interested in dispelling the rumors?" I inquired.

Gaspar frowned. His teary eyes and somber expression pained me.

"Because, Miss Del Valle, Capitan Esteban was a good man. He treated me like a son. I have known him since I was a child, and he was a kind and honorable. Some of us have never recovered from his untimely death. His widow went on with her life as if nothing happened. She is rude, stubborn, and reckless. I believe Eugenia killed him, but no one can prove it. I am just a driver. Ever since the Capitan died, this house has lost its luster. If you are here to help, I want to help you solve the mystery," he offered.

Harry placed one hand on the man's shoulder. "I understand you now," he muttered, "but what of the rumored ghosts? What can you tell us about that?"

Gaspar sighed. He turned the engine on and spun the wheels back onto the roadway.

"Townsfolk murmur that there are ghosts walking the hallways after midnight. The servants are afraid. No one may wander in the hallways after 10:30 p.m. for safety, you understand?"

Harry and I glanced at each other. I shook my head.

"This doesn't sound right!" I remarked.

Gaspar continued, "One can hear the sounds of smashing plates in the kitchen. In the morning the cook finds dishes strewn all over the floor."

I pressed my lips together and listened quietly.

"The east wing is even worse. There. No one is allowed," Gaspar said excitedly.

"Who lives in the east wing?" I inquired.

"Uh, that is the forbidden wing of the house!"

Harry lowered his window. He was feeling warm and rattled.

"Why? Is that Captain Esteban's dormitory?" Harry asked.

Gaspar scoffed. "Ha! No sir! That is the forbidden wing of the mansion; previously occupied by Margarita Del Mar in 1890. She was the young woman who perished in this home. Esteban's betrothed."

My heart fluttered. He said her name; I knew her instantly! Her honey-colored hair, soft-curls, and her invigorating scent: Le perfume de Violette. The popular scent, worn mostly by children, was customary in most homes in Spain because of its delicate composition. It transported me to my home in Toledo where we often doused ourselves from head to toe in copious amounts of that fragrance.

"Who was she?" I wondered. Gaspar had flooded us with so much information that I dared not ask any more. My thoughts of the young woman paused briefly, and I focused my gaze on Gaspar's, who spoke without pause.

"The servants hear footsteps running along the corridor of the east wing every evening and toward the river. Folks around here believe it is the ghost of Margarita running away from her assailant.

"Her assailant?" I gasped. My eyes widened in shock.

Gaspar grabbed a cup filled with ice water and took a sip.

"Yes, the gardener claims a man chased her, but no one believes him. Her body appeared about a mile up the river a month before the wedding. Others say, they pushed her to her death. The nightly screams are heard coming from the veranda, overlooking the cliff into the water. No one has ever seen her ghost, but it is enough to frighten an entire town."

He paused for a moment.

"Is something wrong, Gaspar?" Harry asked.

"No, sir. We're here."

CHAPTER 6

Strangers

We arrived at the Mansion at ten o'clock in the morning. The road, twisting and turning, made me dizzy. The journey felt endless. I wiped my hands on my grey wool coat. They felt warm and sweaty, despite the freezing weather. I would have killed for an espresso or a steaming cup of café con leche, with loads of sugar, for comfort. The events recounted by our chauffeur confused me. Mr. Paladino's betrayal would not go unnoticed. His side eyed glares at his associate, when asked if we were the first investigators, troubled me. My discontent with his handling of this matter was appalling, but for now, treading carefully seemed appropriate. I had to protect Harry.

We reached the black-colored iron bars at the front entrance. Two massive, eleven-and-half-feet tall, arched barriers lavishly decorated opened simultaneously. They sandwiched the gates between nine-foot, white stone pillars on either side. A dense thicket of fifty-foot-tall trees shrouded the long driveway while the home sat back about a quarter mile. Blankets of snow buried all structures, including the drystone fence surrounding the edge of the property, and the trees and shrubs. The clear, narrow pathway towards the fountain, a few feet from the entrance, was magical. Still, the mansion's splendor and natural lush gardens remained obscure. That morning, I watched the vehicle's thermometer plunge to minus three degrees Fahrenheit.

The winters in Virginia Beach paled compared to the brutal climate in Austria. My grey wool coat, with its extra thick layers, barely warmed my bones. It covered my ankles and blocked the wind from my neck. But it was my face buried within my scarves that felt numb and scaly. Harry acclimated to the cold weather swiftly. He stepped out of the vehicle without gloves or a hat. His demeanor cool and collected while I trembled fiercely from the effects of the weather. I never quite understood his tolerance for it, especially with his condition. But he didn't complain.

"Señorita Del Valle, welcome to the mansion!" Gaspar shouted. His excitement was palpable. "In the front row, Señora Victoria Alameda De Cervantes, her daughter-in-law, Eugenia Lines Arguelles De Cervantes, and Natalia Beatriz Cervantes Arguelles, the youngest member of the family. Behind them, Josef, the Butler, last name unknown."

He rolled his eyes. I cringed, stepping forward and eyeing the group awaiting to meet us. I examined the grand structure before me. My gaze rose to the windows and caught the figure of a small child peering at me. Her small body depicted a girl of six or seven. She wore a white gown with her long blond locks tied up in a ponytail. I stepped into one crack between the pavers and stumbled. Both Gaspar and Harry immediately jumped to my rescue. I barreled towards them, but Gaspar caught me before I landed on the floor and made a fool of myself.

"Gentlemen, I am fine, thank you."

Harry crouched down and pulled my shoe out of the crack. He gave it to me. I carefully inserted my foot back into the shoe and straightened my coat. But I wasn't fine. The image of the young child startled me. She was the first ghost I met at the mansion and would be the kindest.

The mansion had pristine walls of white stucco. Elaborately designed and contouring the twenty-foot formation with its steel-black peaks, depicting the shape of a traditional castle. Its tall windows gave way to spectacular views of the entire landscape, including the river. I leaned my head upward in awe and examined the image before me. The structure spoke to me, etched in my soul as if something inside of me returned with a vengeance to reclaim it. Such a strange predicament for a woman like me. Someone who was devoid of anything valuable in her life except my supernatural gift. A gift that led me to a remote location, which upon arrival, felt oddly familiar.

"Is this the Mansion?" I spoke with a wide grin.

"Yes, it is," Gaspar declared. Then he whispered, "Here, let me introduce you."

"Uh-hum," said the tall man wearing a black suit.

His penetrating gaze sent shivers up my spine. His hazel eyes, brown hair, and pale skin were not an attractive combination, but his demeanor invoked fear in the minds of most people who encountered him. He stood stiff as a board He lowered his gaze to peer at us and introduced himself.

"Miss Del Valle and associate, is that correct?"

I glanced at the man towering over me. His lanky build and stern glare reminded me of my mother, ready to pounce on me at a moment's notice. His stone-faced, haughty stare matched the eyes of the woman holding the walking stick standing in the front line.

"I am Josef, the butler," he spoke with a thick German accent.

He turned to the three women standing opposite of us at the grand entrance. An older, earthly, gray-haired woman, dressed in a grey and white overcoat, sat in a wheelchair staring at us. Her gaze floated in Harry's direction and then off into the distance.

"This is our matriarch, Señora Victoria Alameda De Cervantes," he said curtly.

Harry and I approached the older woman with bright smiles and extended our hands to greet her.

"Good morning, Señora Cervantes," I muttered.

She raised her gaze and stared. Her eyes shifted towards Harry and her demeanor changed instantly. She buried her face in her handkerchief. Her eyes narrowed and her cheeks flushed.

"Margarita?" she cried out, "I thought you were dead!"

The woman struggled to contain her emotions. We stepped forward, wanting to apologize for whatever caused her anguish. She placed her hands on her chest.

"Stop!" I heard her say.

Her voice clear and short. She lunged at me momentarily, pushing me out of the way. She crinkled her nose and glared.

"Miss Del Valle, please step away from my mother-in-law. She is not well!" she said sternly.

A pang of shock and humiliation gripped my throat. I stepped away from the woman. Josef continued his formal introduction, but she raised her hand.

"Josef, I will take it from here," she spoke. Her posture stiffened. Her confrontational stance made me quiver. I gazed at her wrinkled face. Her opal-colored eyes and hair as dark as onyx suggested that she had been a beautiful woman in her youth. She was now in her fifties. She lifted her hand to push a grey strand of hair away from her face and tucked it into her loose bun. She was slightly plump but not overly heavyset. Judging by her dark attire, she was still in mourning. She held a walking stick with both hands, leaning sideways until she settled herself in one position.

"I am Eugenia Cervantes, widow of Esteban Cervantes and this is my daughter Natalia," she said, using her cant to point at the young woman.

"The Mansion of Cervantes is my home. I am troubled by Mr. Paladino's decision to invite you here. It is hard to fathom that either of you has the wherewithal to investigate the rumors and solve the mystery. I have no choice but to agree to his demands. I am bound by the terms of the trust

I signed long ago. But I must remind you, that there are strict rules in this home, and you must follow them!"

She raised her hand and wiped her eyes.

"Perhaps this is just another stunt that horrid law firm invented to continue the ghost charade. I assure you; I am not amused," Eugenia Cervantes continued. She blew her nose with her handkerchief.

"Mrs. Cervantes, we are professionals in this field. I do not intend to be a nuisance of any kind. Our presence here is strictly business," I countered.

"That's what they all say, Miss Del Valle, and they accomplish nothing," she rebutted.

She waved us off and turned away, leaving the elder Mrs. Cervantes crying her eyes out, while the young woman attempted to comfort her.

"Josef will handle the rest, I am tired," she said grimly.

The butler motioned for us to follow him into the home.

"This is our staff; I will introduce you later."

He turned away from us. The servants lowered their eyes and nodded their heads. "Everyone, head back to your duties," he demanded. "Carlotta, follow us. I have instructions for you," he said.

We walked silently behind the young woman who was pushing her grandmother in the wheelchair. Everyone else walked behind us.

We entered the first floor of the three-tiered foyer. An enormous sized glass chandelier hung from the ceiling in the center. I looked around the room, stunned by the natural beauty of the staircase leading to the second and third floors. The walls near the entrance were adorned with silver-gold, pink and brown wallpaper and accented with rustic brown sconces. High gloss marbled white floors and custom-built cherry wood fireplace. Every wall in the mansion boasted at least one sconce on each side. The bright rooms enhanced the beauty of the mansion. My mouth hung open for just a second too long. I had envisioned grandeur, but not to this extent.

The ship's luxury paled compared to the décor in this place. There were rare instances in my life where I revered anything. But the mystical ambience in the mansion deserved that and more. I was standing there, mouth gaping and staring at around the room when I felt a pair of chilly hands wrap themselves around my eyes. My body stiffened.

"Miss Del Valle, guess who?" I heard a high-pitched voice whisper.

Harry scoffed. I placed my hands over the delicate hands that covered my eyes.

"Who is it?" I asked.

"It's me," she replied, laughing. "I am the last one left."

She removed her hands playfully. My eyes widened, and I smiled. I turned around to spot the woman and glimpsed her bright eyes and wide grin.

"I am Natalia Cervantes," she exclaimed. "The best and brightest this family offers."

Her dark blue dress stressed her waist perfectly. She was young and beautiful.

"Welcome to our home. I am delighted to have you both here," she added.

"Carlotta, please tend to the guests, prepare hot chocolate and biscuits for them," Josef said in a firm voice.

He walked over to Mrs. Cervantes, who was sitting in her chair, sniffling, and blowing her nose with a handkerchief.

"I will take Mrs. Cervantes back to her suite. Your arrival has unsettled her!" he said curtly. The woman became agitated.

"No!" she shouted. "I don't want to go back there!" she pleaded.

But her pleas fell on deaf ears. He paused, motionless. Nostrils flared. Tight-lipped. Determined. He pulled her wheelchair out of the way.

"If you will excuse me, Mrs. Cervantes needs some rest." He said, avoiding eye contact and disappeared into the adjacent room. I turned to Harry; my jaw dropped.

"What is his problem?" I retorted.

The more I thought about their rudeness, the faster I wanted to run away from there. My body tensed and I shuddered.

"We don't have to stay here, you know." I said, glaring at Harry.

His eyes darted back and forth between Carlotta and me. He walked over to the corner of the room. Then motioned me over.

"Miss Carlotta, please forgive us, but I think Miss Del Valle and I need a private moment," he said calmly.

He stood there, staring at me, playing with his moustache while thinking. I walked over in a huff, my hands flailing in the air, trying to make sense of this scene.

"What?" I squawked. "What are we doing here, Harry?"

I stomped my feet as loud as I could. I wanted them to hear me. I felt confrontational.

"These people are not like us. They are impossible!" I shouted.

I didn't care if they sent me home at that point. Harry watched my hands balled into fists and knew that I was at my limit.

He bent towards me and whispered quietly into my ear, "Chief, we have them. Do not lose your cool."

I gritted my teeth and my eyes widened, "I am not following you at all right now!"

But Harry did not answer me. Instead, he turned away from me and walked towards Carlotta, who was busy watching the exchange between us. She stood there, arms crossed, leaning her torso against the stairwell, watching us argue. This infuriated me, but Harry's stillness surprised me. He reached Carlotta in a second and extended his hand towards her. He shook her hand amicably.

"Ms. Carlotta, please excuse us. It has been a long journey and we are quite tired. If you would be so kind as to show us to our dormitories, we will gladly accept our meals in our individual rooms."

The woman nodded. "Follow me upstairs, or if you prefer, there is a small elevator in the living room leading to the third floor on the North Wing of the Mansion," she said curtly.

"No, the stairs, are fine," I muttered.

We followed the young woman up the stairs into a long hallway filled with portraits over one hundred years old. Harry's room was directly across from mine. I noticed strange locks on every room in that wing. As we approached the rooms, the sconces in the hallway shifted. The lights flickered momentarily. I walked behind Carlotta quietly not wanting to alert her to what I had witnessed. I tapped Harry on the back and pointed to the sconces on each side of the wall.

"Did you see that?" I whispered through gritted teeth.

He nodded and winked at me. Harry suddenly spoke in a louder than usual voice.

"How many rooms are in this mansion if you don't mind me asking?" Harry asked. Carlotta spun around to face him.

"Well, I suppose you are the first ones to ask that question," she said grimly. "There are twenty-four rooms on the three floors of the mansion to be exact. There are four wings in this mansion—east, west, north, and south. Each wing has six rooms. Add six more for the servant's quarters downstairs."

But Harry continued the inquisition. "Who occupies those rooms, if you don't mind me asking?"

My mind swirled. He wants to stay here. He wants to sort this out! I coughed.

Carlotta turned to me and asked, "Are you alright, Miss Del Valle?"

My face blushed. I grabbed my scarf and quickly covered my mouth.

"Yes, just fine." I muttered.

Trust no one, except the driver and cook. I reminded myself. Carlotta stopped in front of a room at the end of the hallway.

"Miss Del Valle, this is your room," she said, pointing at the doorway. "Mr. Jones, your room is across the hallway, right over there. Anni and Franz will deliver your meals shortly."

Harry and I stared at her. I was not sure what to make of Carlotta.

"There is a dumbwaiter lift in the center of the room. You can place your tray inside. Just open the brass door and pull the lever towards you," she spoke. "Dinner is at 7:00 p.m. sharp."

The woman walked over to Harry's room and unlocked the door. I heard her footsteps shortly, heading away from our rooms.

CHAPTER 7

Grievances

It is me! I am running away from someone.

"Mother, help me. Please!"

I ran so fast; I could not catch my breath. My muscles ached. No, they burned from the pain, but he was behind me, chasing me. I felt my white gown trapped between my legs. I stumbled. I fell.

"Quick, somebody help me," I screamed. "Mother, you know what he'll do. Don't you?"

I forced myself to get up and run again. "Is this what you want for me? For us? For him?"

They would not hear my muffled voice and silent screams. "Don't you see him, Mother! Why won't you help me?!"

He came closer. Close enough to smell his breath. Alcohol, cheese! I gagged. The man's shirt was drenched in sweat and a brown substance spewed from his mouth. He kept coming! So close that I saw the knife.

"He's going to kill me, Mother!"

But she turned away. She did nothing to save me from that monster! I screamed! I ran until I reached the edge. The fall terrified me, and the sea swept me away!

"Knock, Knock!" I heard someone say from the hallway!

I woke up and glanced at my watch. The watch registered 9:30 a.m. I spotted my pale blue robe hanging neatly on the doorway of the bathroom. I rose from my bed and quickly threw it on.

"Who is it?" I called out.

"Miss Del Valle, I am your server, Annie. Breakfast for you!"

I scanned the room and approached the doorway. The knob turned clockwise, and the door swung open. A young blond, in her mid-thirties, waited patiently with a covered silver tray.

"Good morning, Miss Del Valle. You fell asleep yesterday after your meal and slept all night. Mr. Jones instructed me to let you rest, with the long trip and all."

I nodded my head. "Thank you," I responded.

The woman placed the tray over my desk and curtsied. I sat on the chair, staring at her while she stood there, motionless, waiting for me to say something. Was I supposed to do that? I didn't know. This wasn't my normal environment—to be well-versed in the rules of the rich. I shook my head.

"No! There will be no curtsies in this room," I said with a mild grin. The woman lowered her gaze and nodded. "Annie thank you for your service. You have been so very kind. Have you seen Mr. Jones this morning?"

"Yes, Miss. I believe he had breakfast in the kitchen this morning with Mrs. Quinn our cook. He headed out to the stables with Gaspar," Anni volunteered.

"I see! There is nothing else I need right now," I whispered.

The woman smiled and left the room. I sat there tapping my fingers on the desktop. Harry was up to something. He had begun the investigation without me. I wasn't sure why, but there had to be a good reason.

Later that evening, dinner was uneventful. It was a chicken and shrimp stew. Delicious but lightly salted, not like my mother's. I prefer my food very salty or very sweet. I looked around the room and glimpsed Eugenia and her pack of fawners. Josef and Carlotta roamed around the room, thumbing their noses at us every time they looked our way. It was quite uncomfortable for me. Harry didn't seem to be bothered. His poker face was better than mine. To avoid the tension, I forced myself to speak.

"Mrs. Cervantes, you mentioned rules of the house yesterday?" I inquired quietly.

She narrowed her eyes and glared at me. Then burst out laughing.

"Ha, ha, Miss Del Valle, I am so glad you asked. Frankly, I did not think you'd remember or care, since you slept through the night on your first day here!" Her face tightened. "At a young age, my mother taught me the value of respect. When one is a guest at someone's home, it is customary to dine with them. Every night."

She shook her head with a nervous twitch. I wiped my mouth with a napkin and placed my spoon on the table.

"Forgive me, I did not mean to offend you!" I replied. She raised her hand with her palm toward me.

"Save your apologies, dear. I don't care, really!" she said dismissively. "Josef, please announce the rules of the house to our guests now," she said, taking a bite out of a piece of bread drenched in melted butter.

The man bobbed his head while seated at the head of the table. The elderly woman Victoria sat in her chair next to him. Her eyes glazed over. She hadn't touched her meal. She seemed under the effects of a substance, quite like those doctors of my youth gave their mental patients. I worried for her, but it wasn't my place to complain, not yet anyway.

But Eugenia's insults rattled me more than I cared to admit. Her obvious disdain toward me puzzled me in a myriad of ways. She didn't know me and yet she hated me the moment she laid eyes upon me. She barely acknowledged Harry at all during our days at the mansion. However, I realized I would be the brunt of her wrath from now on.

"Mother, please refrain from criticizing our guests. It gives me a headache!" Natalia protested, raising a hand to her forehead.

Eugenia rolled her eyes and frowned but agreed. She turned her gaze towards her meal and didn't speak another word for the rest of the evening. The butler took a deep breath and sighed. He spoke with authority.

"As our dame Mrs. Cervantes informed you, there are rules you must strictly follow while you remain guests at the Mansion. Number one. All meals will take place in the dining room at specified times listed in your welcome letter. Number two. The kitchen closes at 10:30 p.m. Number three. Curfew is 10:30 p.m. For your security, of course. We don't want anyone getting hurt," he said, rolling his eyes and choking out a cough. He continued, "Number four. You will make use of your day off on Sunday afternoon after you have joined the family in our traditional mass at the Chapel in the south wing. Number five. Under no circumstances are you permitted in the east wing of the mansion. No exceptions!!"

Harry and I stared at each other. My ears turned red, and my face flushed. Harry noticed the change in my demeanor, and he suddenly spoke.

"Sir, you realize we are here to investigate the rumors of a haunting," he said, leaning over the table. His eyebrows furrowed, and he pursed his lips, waiting for an answer. Eugenia stared at Josef but didn't say a word.

"Well, Mr. Jones, your investigation will take place while observing our rules. In fact, I am surprised that Mr. Paladino did not explain to you. No one, not even Mrs. Eugenia, can access that wing. Only pure bloodline members of the Cervantes family, have access to that part of the mansion. That means either our matriarch or Ms. Jacqueline Cervantes is permitted. And Ms. Jacqueline Cervantes has not visited the mansion since her brother passed away," he protested.

"Mr. Josef, doesn't Miss Natalia have access? She is a Cervantes family member," I inquired.

"Uh-hum," Natalia interrupted, then she pleaded, "Let me tell them the story, Josef, please. Truth is, I am not a Cervantes at all, Carolina. My father only granted me his surname because another man dishonored my mother when she was younger. Isn't that right, mother?"

But the woman lowered her head and kept silence.

"I wanted to tell you right away. It is not a secret in the mansion, and although my mother has chosen not to speak about it, I assure you, Captain Esteban always treated me like a daughter," Natalia concluded nonchalantly.

I didn't know what to say. Eugenia would not look at either of us. She glared into the distance with her eyes glazed over, like her counterpart, the elderly woman across the table.

While I processed the information, Harry muttered, "Mr. Josef, we work after midnight. How are we going to investigate the mansion, if we cannot use our equipment at the right time? Your rules make our investigation almost impossible to complete."

"Mr. Jones, the rules are what they are! If you cannot work around them, what good are you, really?" he said curtly.

I rose from the chair, determined to figure it out.

"It is fine. Mr. Jones and I will be fine. Thank you for your help," I replied, then curtly excused myself and followed Harry into the kitchen.

Over the next three months, Harry and I conducted our investigations in the living room, dining room, and kitchen. Eugenia insisted on having us sit with her until 9:00 p.m., drinking espresso or cordials after dinner. That left us with an hour and one half each evening to photograph the areas and use the recording device. But night after night—nothing! All was silent. Our doors would lock at 10:30 p.m. and Josef would take the keys, leaving us as prisoners in our dormitories until the following morning at 6:00 a.m. when the click of the keys unlocked the doors again.

Three nights a week at the stroke of midnight, the deathly screams coming from the other side of the mansion were deafening. Chains dragged across the floors. Someone pounded on the walls. The sound of heavy footsteps racing downstairs onto the veranda towards the cliff was loud and disturbing. I heard a woman screaming for help. My mind swirled; my gift was failing me. The sounds were impossible to ignore. They seeped into my brain and grabbed hold of me. Night after night, the physical screams outside of my door bled into a mix of visions of the woman screaming that left me exhausted in the morning. I could see what she saw, but I never saw her face. I was sure my mind played tricks on me. Not even Harry understood my visions. He insisted they all ran together as part of one continuous theme. But things got stranger. The little girl often wandered into my room at night, pointing towards the door and showing me a locket with a pale blue stone. The locket held a special golden key. I wracked my brain trying to figure it out, but I didn't know who she was or what she wanted.

CHAPTER 8

Betrayed

Sunday morning after breakfast I stepped into the rear elevator. Avoiding Eugenia kept me sane; she rarely travelled near the staff. My arrival in the kitchen rattled Mrs. Francis the eldest cook, who—I learned—barely spoke German. Victoria Cervantes insisted on keeping the woman at her station, so they set up a clause in the trust barring anyone from firing her. They forced Eugenia to sign.

"Good morning, Mrs. Francis."

The large female in her sixties greeted me.

"Carolina, please call me Genny," she added, grinning. "Besides, you have been here long enough."

I watched her drag around the kitchen while I sat on the table.

"Dear, what would you like?" she asked.

"Uh-hum, Genny!" I spoke. "Forgive me for asking, but Gaspar told me to trust you. I—I am curious."

I struggled to blurt the phrases out. She seated herself next to me.

"What is it?"

"Genny, there's a ghost in this residence and I require answers." I implored, extending my palm out to her. The woman's eyes widened. "I am not just an expert in occult sciences; I am a seer, a mystic, someone who sees ghosts."

Her eyes furrowed, and she gripped my fist. "Jesus, Mary, and Joseph! Child, never speak those conversations in this home out loud!" You'll get killed for that!"

I shook my head. "What do you mean?"

She rose from her chair in a huff. I gazed at her while she traced the sign of the cross on her forehead. She whispered nervously under her breath. Then placed a steel pot of water on the stove.

"Ay, Dios Mío, let's have tea!" she squawked. "Have you told anyone?" she demanded. "Your colleague? Gaspar?"

I buried my head in my lap. "No!"

She stood there, covering her mouth. Her eyes narrowed. I quivered.

"Carolina, be careful! Eugenia and Josef are dangerous!"

"Yes!"

"You haven't informed them?"

I raised my forehead. "I can't! Gaspar instructed me to trust you, so I am!"

The whistling sound from the boiling carafe startled me. She spun around, twisted off the gas, and served two cups of chamomile tea. She sat next to me. Her relaxed, joyful expression returned.

"What do you want?" she asked.

"The spirit of a youthful girl occupies this home," I breathed.

"Do you mean Margarita; the one they killed?"

"No, this young lady is six years old. She wears a ponytail and a golden locket. Do you recognize who she is?" I whispered.

Genny scratched her skull. Her eyes widened, and she remained there, motionless. Her face grew pale as a phantom.

"No, it can't be!" she replied. "You don't recognize Eli. She passed in 1885. The family never spoke of her," she said teary eyed. The woman held her stance. "Are you telling me the specter of Elizabeth Inez Cervantes Alameda, age seven when she died of cholera, still inhabits the mansion?"

I nodded. "The child wants to tell me something, but I don't know what it is!" I declared.

Genny sipped from her cup. She looked around, lost in her thoughts. Then her eyes brightened. "Perhaps she is showing you her favorite locket because she wants you to find it?" She added, "Eli was a precocious child. The youngest of the clan of five children: Julian, Esteban, Jacqueline, Pedro, and Elizabeth. During the Civil War, Coronel Cervantes, the patriarch of the family, travelled to India and parts of South America with a group of soldiers seeking help. Upon his return, and unbeknown to him, he carried the bacterial disease and infected Eli. Coronel Cervantes survived cholera, but the child didn't. He never forgave himself and died of old age, regretting the death of his daughter."

"Where would I find her locket; it has a key. She wants me to have it!"

But Genny shook her head. "No luck, Carolina! Jacqueline Cervantes has the locket, and she is far away in Argentina. She vowed never to return. It is no use!" she said decisively.

I sat there, defeated momentarily. But then I envisioned the child, and I had to help her!

"What if I write to Jacqueline? Do you think she will come back?" I pleaded.

I could tell she felt my desperation because she held my stand still, preventing me from shuddering.

"Very well, dear! Do not mention that you are a seer in your letter! Jacqueline is a kind woman, but you must let her meet you first!"

I nodded. "Genny, one more question," I asked politely.

"Hmm. What now, Child?" she said impatiently.

"You mentioned someone killed Margarita. How do you know that?" I asked.

"I don't know that for a fact, but Mrs. Victoria often speaks of her death as if she knew the murderer. It's not what she says, but how she says it. Her mind is slipping; and she's often heard at night calling for Margarita to forgive him. But who that is, we don't know!"

I pouted. "Any chance it was her betrothed, Captain Esteban?"

The woman immediately shot death stares at me!

"For God's sake, Child. Never speak of that! Capitan Esteban was nowhere near the mansion on the night of her death. He loved her dearly," she sobbed. "He was a kind man."

My eyes welled up with tears. "Oh, Genny, please forgive me, I didn't mean—I was just curious!" Too late.

Josef walked into the kitchen demanding my presence at the chapel.

"Miss Del Valle, rules are rules! Mr. Jones has already made it to the chapel. Why are you still here?"

He watched us both in tears and quickly inquired, "What's going on here? Mrs. Francis, why is Miss Del Valle in tears?"

But I interrupted before she uttered a word, "Mr. Josef, I burned my hand on the stove, trying to grab the tea." I covered my hand, pretending to be in pain. "Would you like to see?"

He scoffed. "No thank you!" he said curtly. "Carry on!"

Genny waited for him to leave and then cracked a smile. "How did you know he would not look?" she asked eagerly.

"Mr. Josef is scrupulous; he hates the image of anything imperfect and distasteful—blood and guts, not his cup of tea," I retorted.

Later that evening, I noticed Harry and Carlotta exchanging glances. Harry had been operating solo recently, and I could not figure it out. He seemed distant. The one obvious clue was his friendship with Carlotta. If I didn't know any better, I would have sworn they were romantically involved. Apparently, Eugenia caught that as well because she didn't hold back.

"Mr. Jones, I have noticed you developed a close friendship with one of our staff. I must remind you, you may not consort with the servants," Eugenia declared.

I sat next to Harry. My mouth wide open. It was the first time Mrs. Eugenia addressed him at the dinner table and left me alone.

"Pardon me, Mrs. Cervantes, I assure you, there is nothing personal going on with Ms. Carlotta," he countered.

But I knew he was lying. The way his eyes twitched. His nervous laugh. He was hiding something. I had always trusted Harry. He was family, but lately, his disappearing acts were bothering me. Trapped in our rooms with our every move monitored by "the creepy duo" was exhausting! But Harry and Carlotta behind my back? That was unforgiveable! I had to come up with a plan soon! Jacqueline would come to the mansion, and we would figure it out together. But that would take at least three months. In the meantime, I needed a seance.

That Tuesday, I met with Gaspar and his friend Otto outside the gates of the mansion. Gaspar translated for me since Otto spoke German.

"We must perform a seance in the room closest to the east wing. I considered the ballroom near the gardens. They monitored our operation. Harry fell prey to Carlotta's charms. Her tight short skirts, flirty eye. Their constant sneaking around. She is a bad influence on Harry. Do not trust him. This must take place soon when most of the servants have left the mansion," I offered.

Gaspar listened carefully.

"Please ask your friend if he knows any practicing witches in town."

Gaspar's eyes widened. He stuttered through his sentences.

"Well?" I demanded.

"Uh—Otto says he knows of one woman. Her name is Ingrid, and she has been a practicing witch for twenty years." I nodded.

"Carolina, do you know what you're doing?" Gaspar asked.

"Yes, Gaspar! You want to help me? Get rid of the servants!"

Gaspar turned to Otto and held his palm up. "Wait here!"

He pulled me aside in a huff and whispered, "How are we going to get you out of your room?" He raised his hand to his forehead and stared at me.

"Let me handle that! Just make sure Harry and Carlotta are out of the house as well."

Gaspar rolled his eyes. "I guess you noticed they are together, huh!" he said, smiling. "Yes, Gaspar, and she is a troublemaker. Love makes people do stupid things, and Harry may have just fallen in love with her!"

Gaspar rolled his eyes again and nodded. "Fine, Chief! Sunday evening?" he asked.

"Yes, Sunday at midnight," I muttered.

CHAPTER 9

Lucy

Malaga 1923

The hospital in Malaga with its austere walls, steel beds, and flimsy mattresses made for a scary stay. The countless screams of patients in their delusional states were enough to turn the sane insane. The morning after the family meeting, mother, accompanied by Father Armendariz, dropped me off in that dreadful place. She barely spoke to me on the way over, and when she did, she said, "This is where you belong. Try to behave."

I spent three years in that hospital. However, my sense of self and spiritual evolution molded into a powerful gift. The four walls shielded me from the rest of the world, but it created a safe environment for me to explore my intuition. This is where I met Lucy, my guide. She prepared me to form alliances with the most unexpected cast of characters.

On my first evening there, I met a woman named Doris. She was the night-shift nurse, whose son was paralyzed from the waist down after a car crash in Seville. Seville, second in line to Malaga in popularity, was also a coastal town. Both formed part of the Andalusian community on the southern coast of Spain. I longed to visit the beach; the thought of being so close to it made my days at the hospital hopeful. Doris became my ally. My guru. My friend.

The first time we met, I told her I knew of her son's accident and predicted that he would walk again. The woman cried. She didn't understand how I knew her secret, but she trusted me. I begged her not to tell anyone of my gift. In return, she hid my medication, allowing me to avoid days spent in a haze like her patients residing with me.

In the first six months of my stay, my mother visited once, but I refused to see her. My friend Leticia sent me letters every month regaling me with the town's latest gossip. My father, too, sent a letter once. A list of regrets, really. His greatest regret: letting me rot in that hospital. Letting my mother win! I didn't respond.

Two years later, my mother informed the hospital that Father passed away. His estate would cover my stay until my eighteenth birthday, but after that, I was on my own. On my eighteenth birthday, the hospital released me into a charity house run by the local church. They claimed they cured me, but I knew the money ran out! My mother wrote to me many letters after that, expressing her regrets. But the letters fell on deaf ears! I was free to be me! She would never see me again, I'd sworn, but life had other plans.

My sister Emma married a scoundrel and moved to the Canary Islands. She bore six children, and from what Leticia relayed to me, Emma was miserable. Her husband barely worked and spent his money drinking in a brothel. Her prospects of a good marriage vanished with Martin's death, and she settled for Lucian. Mother sent her money here and there to help feed the kids, but it only lasted long enough for Lucian to get possession of it. She was miserable.

Lillian never married. She became a nun and opted for a simpler life. She never wrote to me. I suspected she regretted her ways, but she didn't have the nerve to admit it. We left Mother to sell our home and move with her sister, Charro. Both women lived quietly on a small farm and kept each other company. The days of the feasts and social parties evaporated, but they only had themselves to blame. I would not return, I told myself. I would not forgive them.

I sat there, reminiscing about my days at the hospital and how my family had imploded. Then the bell rang, pulling me back to the present. Time for dinner. I got up to grab my grey and black shawl when the sound of a knock startled me. "Who is it?" I called.

"It's me Harry!" he breathed.

"Hold on Harry!"

Poker faced. I turned the knob and opened the door. He stood there with a wide grin, expectant. But I wasn't in the mood.

"Are you ready for dinner?" he said.

"Sure," I muttered. I pursed my lips and avoided his gaze.

"Is something wrong, Chief?" he asked quietly.

I shook my head. "No!"

He rolled his eyes. "Come on, Chief, is it because I've disappeared a few times?" he asked somberly.

"Harry, I don't know what you're up to, but I assure you, I don't like it," I retorted.

"Believe me, I am on your side," he said. "I've uncovered some news. We need to meet later, away from the house." I stiffened.

"Are you seeing Carlotta?" I demanded. Harry paused. He lowered his head and nodded.

"I'm sorry, Chief. I lied to you," he breathed.

"Harry, how could you?"

My cheeks flushed, my heart thumped, and I was furious!

"How dare you engage in a romantic relationship with someone we don't know whether or not we can trust? This is outside of the rules!"

My tears rolled down my face. I sobbed. Was it jealousy or betrayal? I wasn't sure, but his words dealt me a blow. I was gut punched, unable to breathe!

"Carolina, please forgive me for lying to you!" he urged. "Carlotta is a good person; she has revealed many secrets to me, and I love her!"

He grabbed my hand. I pulled away from him furiously.

"Let me go, Harry!" I yelled.

I heard a scuffle down the hall and noticed Carlotta running towards the service elevator. She watched me explode and stood there, smirking. Harry never saw a thing. I settled myself before dinner. I had to go at this alone. With Harry and Carlotta teamed up, she would steer him down a treacherous path if he wasn't careful. I blamed myself for bringing him along, but I needed help to solve the mystery. My ears would indulge Harry in whatever news he gathered, even if what he said might be the sinister workings of a madwoman. But his betrayal blew my heart to pieces and recovering from that seemed impossible to fathom.

That evening, I sat in the living room drinking tea with Eugenia. Her demeanor towards me had softened lately. She sat across from me in her favorite red and gold upholstered chair. Her face sported a small grin.

"So, Miss Del Valle, how is your investigation going?" she asked, holding her teacup over a small flower-printed plate.

"Well, Mrs. Cervantes, I was hoping we could dismantle the rumors of the ghost, but as you know, the east wing remains closed. We have all heard the loud screams at night. In my expert opinion, spirits haunt the mansion," I whispered.

But the woman gleamed. Something very unexpected—as if she wanted to hear that conclusion. I sat up and took a sip of my coffee.

I continued, "You'll forgive my candor, but the happenings in this place are quite concerning." She nodded. "How have you been so strong all these years?"

She took another sip. "So, you believe they are real?" she asked.

"All the evidence points to it."

She set her cup down, grabbed her stick, and stood up. "Huh, what does this mean for us?" she asked.

"Mrs. Cervantes, no one will purchase the mansion once they learn of my review!" I said grimly.

But to my surprise, she seemed delighted. She let a wry smile escape and quickly covered her mouth with a napkin. "When will you finish with your investigation, may I ask?" she countered.

"Soon. I must conduct a few more sessions. Try to draw out the ghost with our equipment. Perhaps you might allow for an exception to the rules. Just one evening, so that we may record at midnight. If we can capture voices, we will solidify our findings with Mr. Paladino and leave the mansion soon thereafter!"

Eugenia walked across the room and waited for the elevator. "Yes!" she replied. "Tomorrow evening, you may conduct your investigation at midnight!"

CHAPTER 10

Conflicted

The next morning, Gaspar and Otto met me by the gardens. Spring bloomed and the sun shone brightly. Natalia and I sat in the courtyard, excused by Eugenia from the tedious breakfast routine at the dining room table. Every morning we sat and stared at each other silently. When Eugenia spoke, it was usually a nasty remark directed at me or the servants. Her nostrils flared and lips pursed.

To make matters worse, Harry's constant flirting with Carlotta during mealtime was beginning to scare me. The passing glances. The way she accidentally grazed one of his body parts with her arms. Harry's illicit romance upset me. Nothing about that relationship felt honest. Their public displays of affection, hand holding, kissing, and hugging when they thought no one was looking was too much for me to bear.

On occasion, Eugenia's rare, but poignant criticisms, triggered painful memories: Mother's abandonment and Father's failure to protect me. They trapped me in a jungle with no one to save me. Yet, I craved that protection. The one Harry afforded me but now had been so easily abandoned. Reminding myself to put one foot in front of the other daily helped to ease the pain.

"Natalia, what plans have you for the weekend?" I mumbled.

"Ha! There is a fair in town and Mother promised to take me!" she gushed.

"My goodness, which is quite exciting!" I countered. "Have you picked out a special outfit for the occasion?"

"Not yet! Want to go shopping with me tomorrow?" she asked.

I broke a piece of bread and spread orange preserves onto it. "Better ask your mother's permission, you know how she feels about me leaving the premises on a weekday."

She squealed with laughter. "Well, leave that to me, young lady, and I will make sure Gaspar is free to take us!"

I smiled. The warm, sumptuous bread melted in my mouth. I washed it down with a hot sip of café con leche and raised my head to feel the warmth of the sun shining on my cheeks. Despite the outside disturbances, this was heaven on earth—the sound of the birds singing, the subtle freshness of the river nearby. How had I been so lucky to be here? A place I had grown to love.

The gardens overflowed with edelweiss flowers, belonging to the sunflower family. Their leaves covered in tiny-white hairs gave them a woolly appearance. The white roses and pink carnations decorated the gates of the mansion. A section of the gardens displayed lavender flowers. Their scent so invigorating, it became my refuge. A tranquil retreat where Lucy would guide me. Sometimes, Eli would join me. She'd offer me a flower. Or sit with me. She knew Jacqueline was on her way, and this made her happy.

Countless times, I had asked Lucy to reveal the name of the mystery man that I had seen in my dreams before my arrival to the mansion. But neither Lucy nor Eli had any answers. It was as if he'd vanished from existence. No matter how much I centered my thoughts and pondered on his whereabouts, there was no answer—a void the size of a vast ocean.

Out of the corner of my eye, Harry appeared. He'd been forced to bear Eugenia's verbal assault today. I didn't mind it. He deserved it all.

"Chief, can we talk?" he breathed.

I shrugged. "Sure."

Natalia eyed us curiously and hurriedly excused herself. "Caro, tomorrow after breakfast then?" she said.

"Yes, looking forward to it!" I countered.

Harry sat on the table. His penetrating gaze upset me. My eyes avoided him altogether. I sat still with my arms relaxed. Somewhere in the back of my mind, I needed to let him speak his truth.

"I know I've disappointed you in every way. I am truly sorry about that. When we arrived, all I wanted was to solve the mystery and Carlotta had information." I squirmed. "She rebutted my charms initially, but soon enough, she fell in love and trapped me under her spell."

I wanted to vomit. The conversation was much more uncomfortable than I could muster. My posture stiffened. I closed my eyes bracing for impact.

"Her father Anthony, the old gardener in the home, told me that the night Margarita died he was present."

"Are you pulling my leg?" I shot a glance at him.

"Yes, Margarita was murdered, but not by a stranger!"

My mind swirled. I felt a pang. That same pang of pain the woman in my dreams felt. The runner. Instinctively I recalled the image of her running down the stairs screaming for help! Harry watched me intently.

"Who killed that woman?" I demanded.

He shook his head. "This has not been confirmed, but Tony thinks it was Esteban's elder brother Julian."

I rubbed my skull. "I don't understand," I muttered.

"Something about jealousy. Julian was married, but he was not his father's favorite. He tried to rape Margarita before her marriage to Esteban, but things went awry, and she died."

"Harry, Carlotta's father knew this and never mentioned it to anyone else?"

Harry placed his hand on my shoulder. "No one ever got close enough to ask."

My mind was swirling. "Don't let the 'creepy duo' find out about this." He nodded. "Eugenia gave me permission to investigate at midnight tonight. Are you free?"

He smiled. "Of course, Chief!"

My face remained devoid of expression. Unmoved. "Great!"

That evening, Eugenia appeared in great spirits. She approved Natalia's request.

Harry cut his boiled egg in half with a spoon. His eyes focused on the meal. "Madam, would you grant me permission to take a day off this week, besides Sunday?" he queried.

"Is there a purpose to your request?"

"I haven't been feeling well. I would like to visit a local doctor," he retorted.

"Well, Mr. Jones, if that is the case, we can have Dr. Mills treat you at the mansion. No need for unnecessary travel," she said dismissively.

"That may be so, Mrs. Cervantes, but I have a certain condition. There is an herbalist in town who specializes in cases such as mine." He stunned her.

"Well, sir, in that case, you may visit the herbalist. But you have a three-hour window, and then you will return to the mansion."

He is sick! What has that fool been feeding him! The urge to tend to him overwhelmed me. But Harry did not need my mother-hen routine. I hoped he would see Carlotta's true colors, but his smitten grin said otherwise.

The Chippendale grandfather clock measuring eight feet tall stood in the living room. Its golden hands struck twelve. According to Ms.

Cervantes, the clock was a family heirloom that had been there since 1805. They pristinely preserved the clock. A contemplative marvel.

Harry entered the room and behind him was Carlotta, eager to help. My impulse to chase her out of the room blinded me. But Lucy had warned me against it. I glanced at her and nodded. Harry seemed pleased with my acceptance. We settled into our usual routine. We turned the recorder on, set up a camera in each corner of the room, and sat down.

"Is there anyone here?" I began the session. "My name is Carolina Del Valle; this is my partner, Harry. Can you tell us your name if you're here with us?"

No sooner had I spoken when the sconces to the left side of the wall moved.

"Ah!" I heard Carlotta scream. "Did you see that?" she said pointing at the wall.

My finger travelled to my mouth instantly. I glared at her, and she moved aside. The lights flickered. Once. Twice. Three times. Harry wrote on a piece of paper. He handed me the writing: "Someone is interfering with our investigation; let's play along!"

I nodded. Carlotta watched our exchange. She stood there clueless but unyielding. The sound of fluttering wings smashing against the window of the living room distracted me. We ran outside to see what it was; Carlotta came with us. A dead crow. Harry stared at me silently and pulled on his moustache. He turned and twisted in pain.

"My stomach!" he cried.

I rushed over to him, but Carlotta beat me there.

"Harry are you well?" I asked.

He writhed in pain. "Chief, I am sick! Can we continue this another time?" His pain was my pain.

"Of course, Harry. Carlotta, quick, take him to his room. Get him some mint tea."

THE MANSION OF CERVANTES

She nodded. Upon my return to the room, the recorder was out of place. The microphone abandoned awkwardly as if someone had left in a hurry.

On the way to my room, I stopped over at Harry's to check on him. She was his girlfriend, but I was still his boss! His deathly appearance sent me over the edge.

"Carlotta, what did you feed him?" I demanded.

She cowered down with her hands over head as if bracing for impact. I wanted to pounce on her and release my rage! Those years of neglect unleashed a volcano of emotions. An unbridled fury aimed at her for stealing my best friend had her shaking. I hurled myself, grabbed her by the hair, and pushed her away from him. She didn't fight me. She sobbed uncontrollably. I paused. Had I become that jealous monster? Rearing its ugly head amid such turmoil?

Lucy called out to me, "Carolina, stop!"

I glanced in Harry's direction and recognized Eli offering him a cup of tea! Her presence centered me. Carlotta sat in a fetal position crying! I stepped towards her and extended my hand. She rose slowly, still shaking.

"Forgive me!" I pleaded. "Harry is very special to me, and I can be overprotective sometimes."

Carlotta wiped her tears and straightened her skirt. "I know you care about him; I didn't know he was sick. At home we always eat pasta with every meal, but now I see that may be the problem."

I shook my head. "Ugh, he didn't tell you that any wheat products will make him violently ill?" I breathed.

"No. Had I known, I would have never!" she countered. "I love Harry; we wish to marry soon!"

I returned to my room and sobbed. Harry, married? I wanted to die. Considering he was so young, and we made plans to travel the world after this adventure. My despair washed over me in waves. The grief was such that I had never experienced anything like it. Was I in love with Harry? No. I loved him as a sister loves her brother, a cousin, or even a father. Yet, my need to protect him knew no boundaries. Carlotta was not right for him. Sooner or later, he would learn the truth. But loving Harry meant I had to let go! Let him be happy.

CHAPTER 11

Seance

That morning Natalia dragged me to several boutiques in town. She settled on an orange and pink dress with a matching bonnet. She accessorized with white gloves and shoes. Her rose-petaled purse was out of the ordinary for a woman her age. It was customary to wear one's accessories in the same color. When we returned home, Josef informed us that Harry was resting in his room. Carlotta had informed him of Harry's condition, and Dr. Mills rushed over early this morning.

"Mr. Josef, do you know if Harry granted Carlotta permission to disclose his diagnosis?" I queried.

The man scoffed. "I haven't the slightest clue, Miss Del Valle, but that is of no consequence. Carlotta acted properly. It is her duty to disclose all pertinent information that becomes available to her directly or indirectly."

"Pardon me, sir, but some information is personal. Medical diagnosis is none of your business," I declared.

His eyes narrowed and he towered over to speak. Natalia interrupted him immediately.

"Josef, please, you're staff here as well. If Miss Del Valle says it is none of your business, then it isn't."

He stiffened. He glared at me but didn't respond. He turned around and departed from the kitchen.

Natalia laughed hysterically. "See that old crow, he is so annoying! I don't know why mother lets him run around this place acting almightier than thou!"

I watched Natalia and wondered how such a lovely woman maintained her positive attitude in the company of those two.

"Young lady," I gushed, "run along and get ready for dinner. I will meet you back here in twenty!"

Genny cooked a special dinner. Seafood paella. My favorite. Josef poured glasses of Spanish Tempranillo wine from the regions of Catalunya, Spain. My tastebuds delighted themselves once again. Our cook had learned of my preference for certain foods and catered to me. She often prepared a separate dish for me: a salty, soupy, yellow rice. To top off this meal, she made tres leches cake for dessert. I indulged in every bite of that cake.

Eugenia seemed anxious. Her hands were unusually shaky. She elevated her wine consumption. Josef made an announcement after he served dinner. His face contorted more than usual. His lips quivered uncontrollably, like a nervous tick. Harry's condition controlled my thoughts. Genny would check on him every half hour. Natalie had denied Carlotta's access to Harry. They forced her to go home to her father, to my delight. No one dared challenge Natalia, not even her own mother.

"Ladies, we have an announcement to make," Josef spoke grimly.

"We?" Natalia questioned.

"Hmm. I meant Mrs. Cervantes has an announcement she would like me to read to you," he said curtly. "This morning we received a telegram. It appears that Mrs. Jacqueline Cervantes Alameda de Hurtado is going to visit us."

My mouth dropped. I knew she'd come, but her response was immediate. I expected her to consider it a while longer. Natalia stood up, her wild curls springing in the air. Her hands clapping.

"Aunt Jackie is coming home?" she let out a high-pitched scream. "Mother, this is the best news! I am so excited; I can hardly stand it!" She jumped up and down and ran circles around the table.

"Child, that's enough!" Eugenia charged. "There's more," she added.

"More? What do you mean?" Natalia stopped at her chair and took a seat.

"A young man by the name of Ariel will accompany Jacqueline." Eugenia gritted her teeth.

Natalia's eyes furrowed. "Ariel, as in her husband's nephew?"

"Yes, what do you know of him?" she asked.

Natalia's reaction changed. Her cheeks flushed. "He is twenty. Her nephew is a medical student in Buenos Aires. Aunt Jackie says he reminds her of dad. In looks, that is!"

"So, Jacqueline has filled your head with ideas about this boy, who she now plans to introduce to us?" Eugenia frowned.

"Mrs. Cervantes, if I may? Did she say when she will arrive at the mansion?" I inquired.

She turned her anger towards me. "I don't see why that would be any of your business, Miss Del Valle. This is a family matter. Besides, I suspect, by the time she arrives, your investigation shall have concluded."

My face flushed. The woman's nasty zingers were hard to get used to.

"Mother, speaking of dad, where is his painting? I haven't seen it in years."

My ears perked up. His painting. There was a painting.

"Well, Nat, that old thing? I removed it years ago," she said calmly.

"That's right, Mother. You removed his painting and replaced it with one of yours!" Natalia countered. "Aunt Jackie will be upset that you removed it without consulting her."

"Well, my dear, Jacqueline no longer resides in this home. Thus, she has no say!"

"Very well, Mother, but I warn you, Aunt Jackie will not be happy about this!"

Friday evening, the screams returned. I thought we had ridden ourselves of the thrice-a-week, ghost-chasing event in the east wing. The more I considered the pattern, the more evident the event happened consistently—Mondays, Wednesdays, and Fridays. This week, however, something was missing. It skipped Wednesday. But why? What was different? If, in fact, this was not a ghost but rather someone pretending to be the ghost of Margarita Delmar, what could have happened to place a kink in the chain? My urgency in resolving the mystery increased. Eugenia wanted to get rid of me before Jacqueline arrived. Why? All these questions swirling in my head left me confused. I wouldn't give up. The answer was closer than ever.

By Sunday, Gaspar and Genny agreed to cover all loose ends. Eugenia, Natalia, and Josef would receive their nightly drinks sprinkled with a sedative. I wanted to be sure they would sleep through the night. Harry decided to spend the evening with Carlotta. Now that he was feeling better, Gaspar gifted them tickets to a weekend show in town. Harry agreed to sleep at Gaspar's place to avoid the drive back to the mansion.

Ingrid and Otto came in through the service entrance. We ushered them through the ballroom entrance. A large wooden table was set up in the middle of the ballroom. Moonlight seeped through the ten-foot-tall windows leading to the gardens down to the river. Ingrid brought three of her assistants with her, in addition to Otto. All in all, we were seven. The seance's purpose was to contact the spirit world and request assistance and discernment on whether malevolent spirits walked the halls of the mansion.

Ingrid lit several candles in a circle around the table. She grouped another set of candles in a V-shape, depicting an ancient sign. Soon enough she laid out a deck of cards.

"Miss Del Valle," she said, "grab the deck and spread it out in seven piles, evenly. This is a general reading to help connect us with the guides and other worldly beings."

I set my intention with each pile, wanting to release whatever spirits lay dormant in the mansion.

"For those of you who can hear me, awaken and help us!" she spoke loudly. "We need to know who wanders the hallways of the mansion."

We heard a rumble on the floor directly above us. I pressed the buttons on my cameras, one by one. "Click, snap, shutter, flash!" The sounds reverberated throughout the ballroom. Everyone watched in awe except Ingrid. She maintained focus.

For the first time, the call to those spirits worked. Spirits surrounded us. They resembled the images of past family members, which hung as portraits in the hallways of the mansion. Dukes, counts, even a prince. His portrait was displayed in the west wing near the sitting room. Gaspar's eyes widened. He shifted in his seat and groaned.

"Shush!" Ingrid scolded. Her eyes focused on the first card. She turned it over and revealed the fool. She shook her head.

"What does that mean?" I asked.

"The fool represents you. You've embarked on a journey, but you don't have all of the facts." I nodded. "The card is a warning. You've been fooled, set up by whoever sent you here!"

My eyes scanned the room for any clues. The ballroom filled with spirits, like grand central station in New York on a busy morning.

Gaspar whispered, "Told you, Chief, don't trust anyone."

I rolled my eyes. "Thanks," I mumbled. "Ingrid please."

"Very well, Miss Del Valle."

The second card is the Five of Swords. She pursed her lips, her fingers tracing the image.

"Once again, this card represents trickery, betrayal, and revenge. You are caught in the crosshairs of someone's sinister plan. Their only goal . . . revenge. A pawn in their game."

I exhaled.

"There's more. Another situation involving a personal betrayal."

My body trembled. Poker faced. But all I could focus on was Harry! He talked me into this, and poof, I lost him!

"Should I continue?" Ingrid queried.

I nodded. My body felt weightless in that chair. I wanted to faint, disappear from the gut-wrenching pain I felt, now confirming the horrible plot that brought us here! My shoulders dropped and my head dove into the palms of my hands. Seeking refuge.

"Are you well, Carolina?" Genny muttered. She rose from her chair to aid me, but I raised my palm towards her.

"Yes, please continue. Just need a minute." Genny sat down.

"The third card," Ingrid paused. Her eyes widened. A gleam of hope. "The wheel of fortune." She smiled. "All is not lost, depending on which cards are next, things may turn up."

But someone stood behind me. Their presence overwhelming. An eerie feeling. Goosebumps! The tiny hairs on the back of my neck stood up. I shivered. I raised my head immediately and spun around, crazed and looking for the figure that spooked me.

"What's wrong, Caro? Who did you see?" Genny shouted.

"Whoa! See? What's going on here, Genny?" Gaspar whispered.

His eyes darted nervously around the room, like a pin ball machine. His nervous gaze throughout the séance quickly escalated into full-on panic mode. They all stared. Ingrid's assistants conversed among each other in German, bewildered by my reaction.

"Is he here, Miss Del Valle?" she asked me.

"Who?" I retorted.

"You do see them, don't you?"

I nodded.

"Have you seen the man in the uniform?"

I shook my head furiously.

"The man you seek is right behind you!"

I spun around, rattled, nervous, and there he was! Watching me, studying me! My heart fluttered. "He was beautiful!"

A man in his twenties with a perfectly straight nose and high cheekbones, chocolate-brown almond eyes, long lashes, and full lips. His black wavy hair parted in the middle while the soft waves framed his face and contrasted his ivory-toned skin. Unmoved, I watched him staring at me. He smiled. For a minute, he and I were alone. The sounds of the others murmuring, calling me were deafening. But I stood, motionless, unwavering. Frozen in time by his gaze. His warmth. Across the room, his energy radiated around me, through me, as if we were two bolts instantly connected. My soul left my body. We met in the middle of the ballroom. His radiance enveloped us. We stood there, the white light, twirled around us in circles. Our bodies rose magically, succinctly.

"Don't send me back to them," I cried telepathically. "Let me stay here with you."

"Carolina, wake up!" Gaspar cried.

"She's in a trance, let her be! You must not wake her; it will soon be over!" Ingrid shouted.

Gaspar barreled towards me like a cannon ball. He gripped my shoulders and shook me as hard as he could muster.

"No!" said Genny, running towards Gaspar.

Ingrid's assistants leaped over the table and jumped on him. They held him back. As soon as he let go of me, my knees buckled. I collapsed onto the marble floor.

"Quick, someone get help." Genny screamed.

"No, No!" Ingrid spoke.

She planted herself between Genny and Gaspar, hands wide open across their chests. "You don't understand what's happening. Carolina is a gifted seer," the woman hissed. "I knew it the minute she entered the room. You must not interfere with the process. If you wish to help her, get her some tea, and let her rest. We are done here for the evening," she declared.

Genny ran after her. "Wait, the session is being recorded, right?"

"Yes, Madam!"

"Then we will do as you say, but I want you to finish the reading. For Carolina's sake!" Genny said decisively.

"Very well, Mrs. Francis! I will release everyone from the room. You and I will finish the card reading. You will return the recording back to her when she has recovered."

CHAPTER 12

Esteban

"Caro, you look awful!" Natalia declared. "Bad night?" she sighed.

"Apparently, my stomach can't handle copious amounts of Genny's paella!" I rolled my eyes.

"Did you vomit all night?" she asked. Her brows furrowed; her mouth lobsided in disgust.

"Nope, just a bit nauseated, that's all!" I countered.

"Annie, pour some coffee. She will need it." Natalia directed.

The woman looked radiant. She wore her locks in an updo, hanging from one side. Her white dress with pink and blue flowers reminded me of the dress I wore to my sister's piano recital at the age of nine. Emma played beautifully then. They say those who are musically inclined tend to navigate life fluidly, gently, and happily. My sister did not fare well in that category. I could not help thinking of her now. In this setting filled with everything a young woman could want, Emma would have been in her element, happy and joyful. It saddened to me think it was me instead of her. Cruelly, she was snapped from the lap of luxury with a man she loved. Her fate stolen from her by the sands of time.

Harry burst through the gates. "Chief, are you well?" He grabbed my hands, trembling. He looked spooked.

"Harry, control yourself. She indulged too much last night—nothing to get upset about!" Natalia offered.

He watched her carefully. His sharp glance startled me. Usually, Harry remained cool in unforeseen circumstances. Whatever Gaspar told him about last night had an effect. It clearly shook him. I pursed my lips avoiding his glance. Then cracked a smile.

"Harry, Nat is correct. Nothing to write home about. I just need some rest," I spoke calmly.

"How's your sugar? Did it drop last night?" he asked impatiently.

"Sugar? Caro. Do you need Dr. Mills to check your sugar levels, because if you do . . ."

I paused. Grabbed her hands calmly.

"Harry is just concerned. When my sugar levels drop, I tend to faint." Natalia stiffened.

"Genny may have mentioned, I fainted last night. I assure you; I am fine. I didn't want to worry anyone, but Harry's demeanor requires an explanation."

"Oh," she glanced back at me. Her gloved hand covered her lips and she gasped. "What can I do to help?" she demanded.

I waved my hand in front of her face. I lowered my gaze and frowned.

"Miss Natalia, please let me take care of Miss Del Valle this morning. I have abandoned her long enough!" Harry mumbled.

"Harry, that's not necessary. I assure both of you; I am fine. Just need a little rest today. Nat, will you excuse me to your mother?" She nodded. "Great. Harry, please stay. We need to discuss important matters, but first. Natalia, how was the fair?"

The girl beamed. She giggled. "It was wonderful. I rarely get out you know. Mother, of course, was insufferable. She hates public gatherings. But I didn't mind at all," she sighed.

Harry and I relaxed and spent the next hour hearing Natalia's stories about the fair and laughing with her impression of Josef scowling at everyone who approached him.

"Oh," she said, "I almost forgot. Aunt Jackie's arrival is in two weeks. Mother is losing her mind. Make sure to tell Mr. Paladino you need more time at the mansion." Then Natalia whispered, "Mother can't wait for you to leave, but you must stay and meet Aunt Jackie."

After breakfast, Gaspar called us into the servant's quarters.

"Gaspar, did you tell Harry about last night?"

He wiggled nervously. "Sorry, Chief, I had to! I know you two are going through something, but he cares for you. I was terrified last night. Forgive me!"

Harry interrupted. "What happened? Why did you exclude me from the séance? I could have helped," he said defiantly.

"You may have, but this was too personal for me to include Carlotta. I don't trust her! I knew she would follow you here and report it back to Josef. So, excuse me, but I am on my own going forward." I scowled.

He huffed. "I see! You don't trust her, and thus, you don't trust me!" he frowned dumbly.

I felt my fury rise again. "Did you know she blurted your medical history to Josef, of all people, and anyone else who would listen?" I shouted. "Her loyalty lies with Josef, our enemy! *That* is the sort of person you plan to marry?"

He glared at me. Shaking. Bewildered. Shocked. "No! Chief, you're wrong! She wouldn't do that to me! *You* told her about my condition. You betrayed my trust, and I'm still here!" he fired back.

"She could have killed you, Harry. Your love for her blinds you to the point; you're willing to eat her poisonous meals just to appease her." He shook his head. "Maybe I was wrong. But she said she loves you, and she needed to know as your partner. Josef did not need to know your private business, and she disclosed it to him."

Harry spun around, scratching his skull. "No one trusts me to make my own decisions!"

Gaspar stepped in between us shaking his head. "You've done it now, sir! Your betrothed and your boss, they're going at it!" he laughed.

I glared at him. My feet struck the ground so hard everyone stopped and stared at us.

"Gaspar!" he shouted. The man crouched down and moved aside. His nervous tick returned. Harry was angry. His cheeks beet red. He spun around and stormed out.

"Sorry, Chief, Carlotta is going to get it now!" Gaspar swore. I rolled my eyes and followed Harry.

That night, all I could think about was the mystery man. Why was he at the mansion? Who was that man; whose soul called to me? An apparition? A figment of my imagination? Had my mind gone mad? The image of us twirling around in the magical light like twin flames was etched in my vision permanently. Despite my anger with Harry, I didn't want to leave. It was the first time that my visions had given me a full glimpse of the man in the uniform.

The others, all here. Why had they kept themselves hidden all these months? My stay was beginning to feel like a box of cracker jacks. Diving slowly into the mix, searching for the treasure to reveal itself. He was that treasure! So were they! My gift had afforded me the light in which to observe the sights of another era and smell the faint odors of cigars and light fragrances of every spirit that whizzed by me. I wasn't alone for the first time. There were many with me, laughing, joking, having a party that no one else could witness.

The sounds of the piano playing Beethoven's Für Elise wafted through the ballroom. The gates of the other side were blown wide open by the séance. There wasn't a better time to be alive then—now being relived in every room. I heard the constant chatter of the men. Some sipped whiskey while their women, dressed in taffeta ball gowns, discussed their plans for the spring ball of 1895. The ghosts of the past filled every wing of the mansion. Eli twirled in the bright blue dress. Her pigtails wrapped in the same blue ribbon that hugged her waist. Her braids swung around with every skip. But my gaze towards the others was limited. As soon as he entered my room and smiled at me, the world collapsed around me. Everywhere I went, his image imprinted in my soul. I wouldn't dare mention him to anyone not even Harry.

CHAPTER 13

Welcome Home, Jacqueline

"A Private Luncheon with Dr. Mills and his wife, 12:30 p.m. on the south wing patio," the note read.

A week flew by quickly, but Mr. Paladino had yet to reply to my urgent telegram. Time was running out, and I had no more excuses to delay my departure. If Mr. Paladino did not step in soon, not even Natalia's good graces could save us. Further complicating things, Harry's relationship with Carlotta had hit a pause. I assumed his discussion with her did not go well, because they hadn't crossed glances in over a week. He avoided her glares at dinner and politely excused himself to his room after our nightly investigations.

I felt awful keeping secrets from Harry, but the trust between us had faltered. My red, rayon dress livened my mood. Although it felt looser these days, it was my favorite dress. A square-buckle belt made of rayon with gold metal holes lining the center matched the décor of the hem of the short-sleeves. I sat down and removed the yellow cloth napkin from the table. While I placed the napkin over my lap, I heard the gruffness of Eugenia's vocals calling on me.

"Miss Del Valle, so good of you to grace us with your presence," she said sarcastically.

Here we go. Poker Face.

Eugenia plastered on a smile, wiped her mouth with the napkin, and settled into an upright position. "Dr. Evan Mills and his wife Olga have been kind enough to meet us for a private affair this afternoon."

"Where is Mr. Jones? Was he not invited to dine with us?" I mumbled.

She let out a sneer followed by a bark of laughter. "Ha, obviously not, Miss Del Valle. God, you're dense! Dr. Mills is here to discuss Harry's condition."

My ears perked up. My mouth went dry. I didn't dare swallow.

"Shouldn't Harry be here? After all, he is the subject of this conversation!"

"We learned through Dr. Mills's report that your 'colleague' is indeed very ill. His condition is serious. As such, his employment in the mansion must terminate immediately!"

I stared at her, dumbfounded.

"Miss Del Valle, Harry has a serious condition. His body's inability to absorb minerals, coupled with his insistence on eating wheat-ladened products, is a recipe for death within the year!" Dr. Mills offered. He crossed his left leg over his right and intertwined his fingers, digging so hard into his knuckles, the white bone was visible.

"Have you spoken with Harry about this?" I questioned.

His eyes narrowed. He leaned towards me with his hands crossed over his lap. "Yes, he knows!" he shrugged.

My wet, dull eyes blinked rapidly. Harry's life mattered more than this house, even if my twin flame remained. A strange gasp escaped my mouth.

Eugenia's face tightened. She paused, "Carolina, it's time to go! Take him back to the States and focus on his recovery!" She moved her chair closer to mine. She placed her wrinkled fingers over my lap. My body shot back, recoiling from her touch. I didn't like how Eugenia made me feel. She looked closely at me and spoke, "We will make arrangements for both of you to return home on Monday morning."

My heart raced. "What about Carlotta? They are going to be married next month!"

The woman's demeanor suddenly shifted. She pulled her hand away. "Don't you know? I made sure they broke off the engagement! There will be no marriage. I want you and Mr. Jones out of Austria. The sooner, the better!" The opal ring on her left index finger turned a deeper black. Her intense, fevered stare shocked me. Dr. Mills and his wife watched the exchange silently; they ate and left shortly after.

My feet jerked upward, sending my chair flying over the pavement. It hit a tree with a rewarding bang. I stared at her, both hands over the table, ready to send the table flying as well. This reminded me of my nine-year-old self defiance, and I would not stand for it.

"May I be excused," I demanded.

Her eyes bulged out of their sockets, but she didn't move out of her chair. "Yes. Make sure to wrap up your investigation by Friday."

Eugenia waved me off. Just as she did with everyone else who annoyed her. "Annie, fix the chair," she called. "Clumsy people everywhere."

The woman remained seated at the table, sipping her coffee and shaking her head. If my feet could fly out of there, they would have. My feet stepped one after the other quickly until they reached the library. I spotted Harry sitting quietly on the yellow and brown velvet cloth couch near the window. He buried himself into the pages of Leo Tolstoy's *Anna Karenina*.

"Does that book interest you?" I asked. He shrugged.

"Eugenia wants us out of here on Monday." I scoffed.

Harry raised one eyebrow and smiled at me for the first time in forever. I dropped into the chair next to him and crossed my legs. I held my arms out as wide as possible ready for an embrace.

"I know we haven't said much to each other, but we need to be a team again." His face beamed.

"Do you still love Carlotta?" He nodded. "She's not my cup of tea, but far it be for me to block your happiness. And Eugenia be damned if she wants to destroy your happiness!"

He stood up, slammed the book shut, and extended his arms to me. His embrace, warm and tender, made me burst out in tears of joy. I never wanted to let him go, but his heart belonged to someone else.

Harry pulled away from me. He stiffened. "You were right. She betrayed my trust. How can we marry after that?"

"Ugh, can't believe I am saying this, but you should forgive her!" His eyes brightened. My chest felt lighter. "Everyone deserves a second chance. Even her!" I rolled my eyes.

He shuffled towards the piano and sat down on the bench. His hands magically poised struck the first key. The loud cadence reverberated throughout the library.

"Johann Pachelbel's Canon in D Major! Great choice," I shouted over the music. Harry sported a wide grin.

"May I?" I said, pointing to the seat.

"Sure," he said. As he played the tune, my heart fluttered with excitement. Despite recent events, we managed to patch things up. We were great!

"No matter what happens! Don't ruin your life by giving up on love," I reminded him.

His eyes focused on each keystroke—his fingers gliding over the keys, like a soft wind over the rolling hills.

"You think this could be our wedding song?" he asked gleefully. But I didn't answer. Baby steps was all I could muster. Wedding song selections were beyond the scope of my abilities. And Harry knew it. He didn't push me. My fingers thumbed through the music books on top of the piano.

"Did Eugenia tell you about my prognosis?" he sighed.

"She's using it as an excuse to oust us from Vienna!"

The music stopped abruptly. He rose from the chair and pulled a silver box of cigarettes from his suit pocket. Smoke filled the room. Too close. My throat tightened and I let out a loud cough. I pulled a pink handkerchief from my white leather purse and covered my mouth.

"Our presence threatens her livelihood. Why else would she want us out of here?"

"I contacted Jacqueline and urged her to come here! She arrives next week. Whatever she has to say, Eugenia doesn't want us here!"

Harry paced nervously around the library. His hands wrapped around his back in a knot.

"There's much you haven't told me!" he said.

"I know. Mr. Paladino is the only who can save us now. My telegram arrived two weeks ago, but he has not responded. After what I did in the garden just now, she's definitely going to kick us out."

He stared at me puzzled by my secrecy. As I explained to him about my altercation with her, someone interrupted the conversation. *Knock. Knock.*

I stood up and called out, "Come in!"

The door burst wide open. Natalia stood there, labored breath, her hair disheveled. Her black and brown coat half open, buttoned incorrectly.

"Hurry, both of you! We have visitors, follow me to the main entrance!"

The walk toward the front door seemed endless. We skipped the service elevators and ran down the stairs, shocked and bewildered.

"Mr. Paladino arrived to save us!" I warned Harry.

"Maybe, let's hope so!"

To everyone's surprise, Gaspar opened the doors of a new vehicle. The black Mercedes Benz boasted tinted windows. The identity of the visitor remained hidden. We lined up by the fountain expectant but worried.

Our fate at the mansion dangled by a thread. Gaspar, cheerful as always, opened the backseat door. A young man stepped out of the vehicle. He wore a grey wool coat, dark shoes, and a grey wide-fit ivy cap, behind him stood a woman in her sixties.

Thump. Thump. Thump. My heart skipped three beats in a row. A wave of emotions coursed through my veins, up to my throat like a volcano ready to erupt into tears of joy. Her presence evoked in me a flutter of elation so powerful I wanted to scream or rejoice louder than anyone on earth! She heard my call and came to save us!

The woman's brown suede hat, tilted to one side, covered her face. Her grey hair and dark eyes mirrored her mother. She grinned at Natalia. The young woman moved about waving her arms in the air, all the while giggling. She ran forcefully toward the visitor.

"Aunt Jackie," she called. The women embraced warmly. Her companion, a man in his early twenties, stood there and waited for an introduction. Josef stepped forward to greet the visitors. His arms hanging by his side, voice cracking—a futile attempt to remain relevant.

"Ms. Jacqueline, welcome home!" His shaky hands extended out to her, but she flicked her hand in front of him!

"New sheriff in town," I mouthed to Harry. He smiled.

Jaqueline scanned our row. She picked up her long skirt and stepped closer. She handed her umbrella to the young man beside her and peered at us intently. We stood behind Eugenia and the elder Mrs. Cervantes, along with the servants. She eyed me carefully, then moved to Harry but didn't say a word.

"Mother," she called, "how have you been?"

The elder woman stared into the distance, like a zombie. Her blank stare and copious amounts of drool left Jackie feeling concerned.

"What is wrong with my mother?" she inquired. Jackie's glare, tight jaw, and bald fists aimed in Eugenia's direction.

"God, I love this woman!" I mumbled.

The onslaught of insults that Eugenia subjected us to paled in comparison to the world of hurt Jacqueline was going to put on her. I hoped. "Anyone, please wipe Mother's face for God's sake!" she demanded. She walked toward us. "Josef, I do not have the pleasure of meeting these two. They are clearly not servants as they are wearing normal clothes!" She towered over Harry and me. The woman was tall enough to tower over everyone in the house except her nephew and Josef.

"What is the meaning of this?" she demanded.

The sight of Josef and Eugenia being visibly shaken was unforgettable. Jacqueline ruled the roost, and they knew it! The urge to laugh consumed me. Harry displayed a wide grin.

"Uh-hum," Josef coughed. "Ms. Jacqueline, this is Carolina Del Valle and her colleague, Mr. Jones. They will be leaving Monday," he mumbled.

She eyed him carefully. Her facial expressions, masked by her enormous hat, made it difficult to decipher her thoughts. She paced slowly around Eugenia. Her eyes on the woman, inspecting her every move.

"Who decided they are leaving on Monday?" she inquired.

"I did!" Eugenia spoke up. Her defiant gaze and hostile voice seem to mentally justify her actions. But Jackie withdrew her fire.

"Well, if you decided they're leaving on Monday, there must be a good reason. We will discuss it over dinner," she countered.

Jackie relaxed her posture and motioned everyone to follow her into the home. The young man grabbed the wheelchair and pushed Victoria behind her. What? Harry and I were scared. What if she did not want us there! I was sure there would be a battle. No. A war! Was I so wrong in my perception of Jacqueline? The battle of the Titans quickly evaporated before my eyes. Instead, we were received with civility and a ladylike discussion over dinner!

We followed the procession into the mansion. A wave of heat engulfed my neck shooting up my ears. I was on fire! Eugenia's defiance burst my bubble. No. She flattened me into a pile of rubble. My dreams of hope with Jacqueline's arrival vanished forever. Jacqueline stood briefly in the foyer. She looked around the room quizzically as if she'd been away for more than a century. Everyone rallied around her, the center of the universe as far as we were all concerned. She took her coat and hat off and pawned them off on a woman in her mid-thirties.

"Gladys, take this to my room. Have the cook come up in five minutes." The woman nodded and left the room. "Ha! I see you've changed a few things around here," she retorted. "This is my nephew, Ariel; he is my eyes and ears."

While the visitors settled, Harry and I joined Natalia in the living room. Natalia called me over to the parlor adjacent to the living room.

She whispered, "So, you and Harry made up, huh!" She winked and smiled wryly.

"Oh yes, Nat, we're good," I replied.

She snorted and laughed. "Did he get rid of the 'pick me, girl'?" she asked.

I frowned. My nose wrinkled. "Pick-me-girl?"

Natalia swayed from side to side. Her hands clutched tightly.

"Do you mean, Carlotta? She's pick-me-girl?" I smiled.

Natalia grabbed my hands and twirled me around in circles. One. Two. Three.

"Yes, silly. You know, 'Pick-Me, Pick-Me!'" We both burst out laughing. "I've never heard that term before."

"That's because the servants gave her that nickname. Nobody really likes her!"

Ariel interrupted us, barring me from making any further disparaging comments about Carlotta. Ariel came downstairs first. Then Jacqueline's personal assistant accompanied her down twenty minutes later. Natalia's demeanor softened when Ariel entered the room. Their energy was invigorating—like yin and yang. As soon as I met the young man, his energy shocked me. He was a perfect match for Natalia.

"Pleasure to meet you, Miss Del Valle. I have always been interested in experiments involving occult sciences. My uncle thought it best that I devote my studies in the medical field, though," he declared.

"Cardiology?" I blurted out.

"Yes, how did you know?" he smiled.

"Wait, Caro, I didn't tell you that?" Natalia scoffed.

"I know. Just instinct, that's all!"

Jacqueline entered the room. She wore her hair short and curly. Her eyes were so familiar.

"Did someone mention cardiology?" she interrupted.

Natalia ran over and put her arms around her. "Yes, it was Carolina. Our resident expert on ghosts!" she smiled.

"Please, everyone, sit."

Jacqueline called me over once everyone sat down! I straightened my skirt and coughed. I sat next to Jacqueline while she fiddled with her rings. Twirling and twisting, her left ring first then her right one. I noticed she wore a man's ring on her right index finger with a square, sapphire stone in the middle with a thick silver band. She barely looked at me initially.

"Miss Del Valle, you look awfully familiar. Someone I knew a long time ago!"

"Who is it, Aunt Jackie?" Natalia mumbled.

"No one you know, my precious!" Her somber look overwhelmed me.

"Oh no, Aunt Jackie, no sadness tonight, please!" Natalia pleaded.

"Mrs. Cervantes, your home is lovely!" Ariel said.

His eyes watched Natalia's every move. They danced in a lover's circle waiting for one or the other to move! Natalia gushed with every response she gave Ariel. The shy woman I'd never met reared her countenance as soon as he showed up. Jacqueline's perception of the lovebirds matched mine. She stared at them, her eyes beaming. She struck me as a kind woman whose suffering had made her strong as steel.

I looked around the room and felt the house alive. Both the living and the dead surrounded us. His spirit appeared next to Jacqueline and smiled. He must have been her brother Esteban. There was no doubt it was him. Both had an identical resemblance to one another. The home contained hundreds of souls trapped after their respective human passing. Jacqueline looked over in my direction. She followed my gaze towards the space above my left shoulder. She smiled. His presence was overwhelming. Her stomach fluttered with butterflies. The house never felt more inviting, more alive.

"It has been ten years since I left and yet the house looks the same, with the exception of a few things!" she scoffed.

At dinner, Eugenia appeared tense. Carlotta, Annie, and Franz served dinner. Annie placed a silver tray of roasted lamb chops in the center of the table after serving each of us a healthy portion.

Tonight, Josef sat elsewhere. He flanked Eugenia frequently. He guarded her fiercely. Jacqueline would not tolerate his intrusions going forward. Josef was calm and apologetic at every turn. The docile version was nonexistent in the five months since our arrival at the mansion. But this Josef was the best form of entertainment.

Jacqueline was quick witted and short tempered when dealing with the creepy duo. She was kind and docile with everyone else, including Harry and me. The tides had turned in the Mansion of Cervantes.

"Eugenia, now please indulge me in the latest developments of the investigation!" she said aptly.

"Well, my dear, there's not much to tell, really. Miss Del Valle and Mr. Jones have determined that my house is haunted. Thus, they were preparing to conclude the investigation by Friday and depart on Monday morning!" she said curtly.

Jacqueline took a sip of her red wine. She turned her gaze towards me and inquired, "Is that true?"

"Well, Mrs. Cervantes," I explained.

"*Jacqueline*, dear!" she interrupted.

Eugenia rolled her eyes, upper lip tightened, nostrils flared.

I laughed. "Well, Jacqueline, it is true. The home is haunted. We have heard the screams of a woman running through the hallways, dragging some sort of chain, and pounding on the walls."

"What?" Jackie squawked. "That's impossible!!" she declared, "This has been my home for longer that I can remember. Never!—and I mean that!—has there ever been such a thing. The whole thing sounds preposterous!"

But Eugenia defended her position. "Yes, my dear, but your residence in the mansion expired ten years ago! You know nothing of the comings and goings of this home!" She coughed, covering her mouth with her hand.

Jackie's eyes narrowed. Her lips tightened. She paused for a moment, then spoke, "This is and has always been my home, Eugenia. How dare you insinuate that I know nothing about this property. It has been in my family for over one hundred years. You are a late comer! An impostor! A nobody! My brother married you because of your unfortunate situation. Natalia, please forgive me, my dear!"

Jackie's voiced raised as she pointed at Eugenia. Her tone turned angry, "How dare you question me in my own home. Once I sell this home, you get nothing." She paused.

Eugenia started to cry. The situation turned uncomfortable.

Jackie faced me. "Carolina, is that all you have? Where's the evidence of the haunting?" she demanded.

But Harry interrupted. "Uh, Ms. Jacqueline, we haven't been able to access the east wing. That is where the activity is coming from," he said nervously.

"So, you need access to the east wing?" she declared.

"Hmm, yes we do!" he said calmly.

"Carolina, do you agree?" she said staring at me.

I nodded. I took a sip of wine. The food was delicious, and I wanted to dive in, but Jackie's confrontation with Eugenia left me so nervous my stomach shut down.

"Ugh, this is preposterous!" Eugenia said. "You're willing to risk their lives with the malevolent spirit haunting the east wing?" she shouted.

"Carolina!" Jacqueline called.

I put my fork down and placed my hands on my lap.

"Honestly, I would welcome it. We haven't been able to conduct our investigations at midnight the way we are used to," I said somberly.

"Damn you, girl! I let you conduct your investigation as you asked. What is this insolence!" Eugenia glared at me furiously. She slammed her hand on the table and pushed her plate away. Everyone stopped eating for fear the battle would turn violent.

I turned to Jacqueline. "Yes, that's true, but it was only once after I said that I believed the house is haunted."

But Eugenia had enough. She grabbed her cane and stood up. "Help me, Josef?" she grunted.

The sight of Eugenia struggling to get out of the chair, flustered and powerless, made me sad. I hated the woman, but she was visibly upset. I didn't want this. No matter how cruel she was toward us, her pain was palpable. Whatever her struggles, she clearly felt marginalized. She walked toward the elevator.

"Not so fast. You and I have more to discuss. Why is my mother in this state? What have you been feeding her?" Jacqueline stood up, rubbed her mother's shoulders, and kissed her forehead. "Mother, I am going to take care of you. Josef, call Dr. Imbroglios in the morning."

Josef stiffened, bracing for impact. "He's no longer the family doctor," Josef replied.

"I don't care! Call him or else!" Jacqueline demanded.

Eugenia remained silent. The onslaught of insults and recriminations started early this time around. Eugenia glared at her sister-in-law in disbelief.

"One last thing," Jackie shouted toward Eugenia. "Why have you dismantled my family's portraits. Mother, Father, Esteban, and mine?"

Eugenia sobbed. She whimpered, trapped between the wall and the elevator door. Everyone sighed in unison. No one expected Eugenia would suffer a blow so early on, but the women's resentment toward each other was fierce. I wondered what made Jackie depart from the mansion.

"Aunt Jackie, I think that's enough," Ariel interceded. "There will be time to sort this out."

"Yes, please, Aunt Jackie. I warned Mother you'd be displeased about this, but she wouldn't listen to me." They both grabbed Jackie's hands and tried to appease her. "I think we can all use a break," Natalia pleaded. Jacqueline nodded.

"You're free to go!" Jackie waved her off.

Eugenia entered the elevator and disappeared.

CHAPTER 14

Rebirth

"Mother isn't feeling well!" Natalia muttered.

She sunk into a white chair, sandwiched between Aunt Jackie and Ariel. Ariel caressed Natalia's hands lightly and tickled her fingers. The pair of lovebirds got along quite well from the get-go. Jackie rolled her eyes.

"I've arranged for you to give my nephew a tour of the property," Jackie declared.

Ariel grabbed a green apple from the fruit basket. He took a big bite, chewing quickly. *Crunch.* He repeated. The sound of his teeth crumpling the flesh of the fruit soothed Natalia. Natalia peeked over Ariel's shoulder, grabbing my hand behind the back of the chair with her white glove.

"Elena will accompany you. Miss Del Valle will stay here with me," Jackie continued.

Natalia squeezed out a laugh, "Absolutely!"

The budding lovebirds finished their breakfast and headed out with Elena, Natalia's chaperone. It was a pleasant morning. Gladys stood next to Jacqueline holding a white umbrella while blocking the sun from her face. This garden scene repeated itself in my memory, like a movie reel. Except, the players were different. Strange faces gnawing at me. Jackie's blank stare suddenly shifted in my direction. I picked up the fork and stabbed a slice of ham.

"Carolina, did anyone mention Margarita's death?" Jackie whispered.

I dropped a mouthful, then quickly wiped the chunks off my face.

"Uh-hum, madam, her death is the reason we're here. To be honest, I don't believe her spirit haunts this mansion."

Jackie's eyes furrowed, she removed her glasses and wiped them off with a napkin. She placed them back on her face and leaned closer. Harry took a sip of coffee and watched her hand movements.

"We hear the sound of a woman screaming thrice per week. But I believe it's a hoax!" Jackie lowered her glasses and peered at me over the rim.

"Now I'm confused," she replied. "You both said earlier that you believed the house is haunted." She added, "How can it be a hoax?"

"Ms. Jacqueline, can we trust you?"

She scratched her nose. A bee flew by her, she swatted at it, sending the bee away.

"Yes, Harry, of course, this is my home," she said quietly.

But Harry sat there, twiddling with a box of matches on the table. His grey suit pristine as usual.

"Jackie, I wrote to you because Genny said I could trust you!"

The bee returned, buzzing so loudly, she blinked her eyes furiously. Her focus re-centered on the conversation.

"You can. Now speak up!"

I hesitated. "The truth is—I am a seer. Not just a paranormal investigator."

"Huh!" she frowned, "I see!" The woman dropped her gaze and drew invisible circles over the table with her ring finger. "What exactly is a paranormal investigator?" she asked, holding a cup of coffee with both hands. She blew over the cup, watching the steam bend, this way, that way—following the direction of the wind. Sip. Blow. Sip. Blow. She put her cup down and grabbed my hand.

I groaned. "Ugh!"

Visions of a young woman from the past, modeling a red and black dress, obstructed my current view. The man of my dreams enters, complimenting her dress.

"You'll be the belle of the ball," he reminded her. Beside her stood an older man in uniform reading a newspaper. Dated April 15, 1895. With her wavy, jet-black hair flowing over her shoulders, she leaned and kissed the man."

I blinked.

"What is it, Child? Tell us."

Harry grabbed my shoulders; he shook me lightly. "Chief, wake up!" He pulled out a small brown bottle, dabbed a cotton napkin with it and brought it up to my nose.

Ugh, the pungent odor. My vision adjusted. The woman's wrinkles returned with a fury.

"Jackie," I hugged her.

"Child, what has gotten into you?"

I gleamed. "Do you remember the black and red dress you wore at the Spring Ball of 1895?" I asked.

The woman's features settled into a frown. A curled string of hair tickled her nose. She let out a puff of air, upwards. The string came back down and again settled over her nose.

"I'm confused," she countered. "Did you see the picture of me in that gown?" she asked curtly. I smiled. She pulled away from me, shaking her head. "What is this? Trickery?"

Her response startled me. The sound of my voice lost somewhere. Harry watched the exchange and lit a cigarette. He blew his match out and tossed it in the trash receptacle next to the bar.

"No, Ms. Jacqueline, there are no pictures of you in the mansion, that we could see! Carolina must have seen you in the dress when you touched her!"

She stood up. "Impossible, young man, even if she had seen me, there is no way for her to know I wore that dress to the ball in 1895." She turned away from me, heading towards the mansion.

"I saw your f-a-t-h-e-r," I meant to say. But she didn't care. Harry tried to convince her, but she left us sitting there. His charms only worked on Carlotta these days.

"Gladys," she called, "I'm ready for music!"

"Harry, it was her! She was there with the rest of them."

"How so, Chief? Does this have something to do with the séance. Your trance?"

I nodded.

"Oh man, let's hope this doesn't get us fired sooner than we thought!" he answered.

That evening after supper, Ariel came to my room. He knocked on the door. I watched the rain pouring down the windows and heard the pitter-patter on the shingles.

"Sure, come in!" I yelled from desk near the window.

"Carolina, my aunt requests your presence on the east wing."

My feet scrambling nervously, I rushed towards my shawl.

"Let's get Harry!" I whispered.

"No, just you. She insists!"

He shut the door after me and walked briskly behind me. Harry was not there anyway, I later learned. He had made up with Carlotta and had gone to town with Jacqueline's permission.

The hallway leading to the east wing was quite different from the rest of the mansion. She removed the photographs hanging on the wall. The stains marked the wallpaper. She preserved the wing, in its same state since May 1895 after Margarita's death.

Gladys lit the brass sconces and blew against the lit match. My heart thumped faster than ever. Jackie waited for me with Elena at the end of the hallway. She wore a long white gown covered with a paisley design in red and yellow satin. Her neck sported a long gold necklace with an aquamarine stone on the outside of a locket. My eyes beamed. Eli was right. The locket was the key to the east wing.

The older woman smiled at me as I approached.

"Come here, my child, forgive me for my misgivings. Your confession startled me," she said somberly. Her teary eyes, and warm smile surprised me. I was sure this was the kiss of death after my raw display of emotion. "Genny told me about you!" she added. "Your striking resemblance to an old friend and your memory of my dress disconcerted me in many ways!" she offered. "Your eyes, your hair, they are different, but something about you remains the same. My mind is old and maybe crazy, but it doesn't hurt to check."

She introduced a different key into the hole, turned the knob and with a click, opened the door. Elena lit the sconces.

Dust filled the air. A musty scent wafted into my nostrils. We both coughed in unison. Elena walked towards a brown oak storage bin, inserted the locket, and lifted the lid. Three paintings lay flat—one on top of the other. She pulled the first picture and showed it to me.

"That's you, I mean, the woman in the red and black dress!" I whispered. She smiled.

"Yes, my dear, this was the infamous ball of 1895."

But I could not help myself. "I know, I remember!" I blurted out.

She gasped then pulled another picture out of the box, held it close to her breast, and wrapped both arms around it. She sighed and kissed the frame. Her tears rolled down her face.

"Carolina, I want to show you something. This is a picture of my best friend. If you truly have a gift, tell me what you see."

She slowly turned the picture over. The image took my breath away. I choked. I grabbed the painting with both hands and stared at the image.

My jaw dropped. Sweat rolled down my forehead. The range of emotions coursing throughout my body stung me like sharp knives, striking me all at once. I shook my head.

"She's me! I'm her!" I mumbled. I covered my hands with my mouth and dropped the painting. My eyes gazed at Jackie; we embraced.

"Maggie!" she shouted, "My best friend in the whole world. How are you alive again?"

I sobbed uncontrollably. "I'm not sure!"

My mouth barely squeezed out a sound. Such a difficult life, only to learn the truth. My soul resided elsewhere in another time. The thought of it overwhelmed me. We faced each other.

"Your brother! He's still here. I mean, his spirit—his soul—is still here. With me!"

Jackie pulled away. She recoiled. "My brother is dead. He cannot be here! I called for him so many times. He never came. Could he have reincarnated like you?" she asked.

I shook my head. "Esteban is here. He was lost in this wing until a séance woke him up!"

Just then, an apparition appeared. Esteban watched us, smiling. Jackie spun in circles looking for him.

"He is still here, Jackie. I promise. So is Eli!"

The woman sat down and sobbed, her hands over her eyes. She sighed and gasped for air.

"My sister. Incredible!" she offered. "What else do you remember? Do you know who killed you? Or him? Was it Eugenia?" she demanded.

"Well, no. I barely remember running but I—I still don't know what happened to me. Someone was chasing me, and Mother wouldn't help me!"

Jackie scratched her skull. "Mother?" she eyed me strangely.

I grabbed a chair and sat beside her. "Yes. Was my mother here when I died?"

But Jackie got up from her chair abruptly. She shook her head and paced awkwardly around the room. Her hands on her waist. She pursed her lips briefly and spoke.

"No, Maggie. The only ones here that night were my mother and Julian! My brother Julian!" she gasped.

I heard his name for the first time. J-u-l-i-a-n! The images flashed quickly through my head. My body swayed back and forth. Knees weak.

"Jackie, I am in a bed. Unable to move. Mother and Julian gave me tea. But I can't move. I scream but no one hears me, not even her!"

"Maggie, what's happening. Tell me. Who did this to you?" she demanded.

Beads of sweat covered my upper lip. The vision was so real that I stuttered to get the words out.

"Mother?!" I blurted out, "She let him hurt me and throw my body over the cliff. I never had a chance. Those visions of me running are wrong! They confused me by the actual events in the mansion. But I never ran down the stairs. I wanted to but the sedative was too strong. He carried me all the way to veranda and threw my body over!"

Jackie pounded her fists against a cream-colored quilt laying over the back of the chair.

"Bastard!" she said. "My brother Julian was a drunk and a male chauvinist. But murder?" She shook her head. "What if you're wrong, Maggie? Maybe your visions are confused," she said angrily.

"No, dear friend! He did it and mother helped."

She cursed under her breath. The vein on her neck visibly throbbing.

"I love you, Maggie, but this can't be! Mother is not a murderer. She couldn't have aided Julian in killing my brother's betrothed."

But I knew this time, I was right. My posture stiffened. I lowered my gazed and wondered if my disclosure was appropriate. After all, this was a shock to me, and as much as Jackie was a good person, she had a right to get defensive. She rose from her chair and her mood shifted. Whatever had made her angry now dissipated.

"Look," she said, "if this is all true, Mother is the only one who can give me answers. I want to trust you, but these are serious accusations and I—I am not sure I believe you!" she finished somberly.

I nodded.

"Let's take a break for the evening, and we will resume this conversation soon!" she muttered.

We left the east wing, both in tears and exhausted.

CHAPTER 15

Belle of the Ball

A month went by. Harry's wedding to Carlotta remained the talk of the town. Although intimate, preparations for a special feast spread quickly. Jackie and I spent time together but avoided discussions of my reincarnation. We carried on as usual in front of the others. One thing was clear, I was Margarita Del Mar. My memories returned slowly. Jackie's presence unleashed an avalanche of visions and a foreign identity I never considered. Esteban's undying love for me solidified my belief that the soul transcends into another realm, only to be reborn again. Esteban, surprisingly, was the exception. His soul refused to transcend, hoping to find me and reconnect. I sat at the dinner table biting my bottom lip, pondering the meaning of life and all that transpired since my arrival at the mansion.

Carlotta managed to behave for Harry's sake. With Jackie's return, everyone in the mansion catered to her wishes. Some acknowledged Eugenia, but even the lowliest servants ignored her loud and obnoxious banter. Josef became the gopher, schlepping orders from Jackie daily. Eugenia withdrew into her quarters most of the day. Her occasional appearance at lunch and supper rarely fared well for her. Jackie's usual animosity was beginning to wear on her. Adding insult to injury, her relationship with Natalia became strained when Ariel was overhead discussing a marriage proposal with Jackie.

"Over my dead body!" Eugenia declared.

"But mother! We love each other!" Natalia urged, "You could move to Argentina with us and let Aunt Jackie sell the mansion, once and for all!"

The arguments were heard often. Neither of them budged. I knew the outcome. Eugenia would lose the argument eventually, but she was a stubborn woman. Not even Jackie could wield her magic wand around that subject.

That evening, the dinner table was pristine as usual. Large glass vases, filled with pink and white roses in a row of three, formed the centerpieces. White linens, contrasting with an embroidered, cream-colored appliqué, adorned the table. Everyone sat at his or her respective places. Josef poured champagne to toast the lovebirds. For the first time, Carlotta joined them as a guest. Eugenia was livid. Nostrils flared; upper lip tightened. She barely acknowledged their presence. And when she did, her head tilted to the side, letting off a deep sigh.

Harry held his fiancée's hand and kissed it softly. Mutual winks and smiles were exchanged between the love birds all evening. His meliorate appearance gave me hope. Going forward, his prognosis would be much improved. Contrary to the doom and gloom show that Dr. Mills presented, Harry gained twenty-five pounds that month, filling out his striped, blue suit. Obviously smitten with Carlotta, he would do anything for her.

Carlotta wore a knee-length, short-sleeved lilac dress. Her neck covered up with ruffles. Her bright lipstick left him looking like a clown every time she kissed him. It was clear someone had forced her to cover up. She sat there, hunched over, incessantly scratching her neck and trying to pull her dress up. Modesty was not her strong suit. But she sure was pretty. No wonder he fell for her. Harry held her right hand and presented her with a pair of diamond earrings as a wedding present.

"Jackie and I picked it out together," he said. The entire scene repulsed me. I reminded myself that he needed my support. Besides, my rekindled romance with a ghost meant everything. Relieving our memories brought me great joy. Sure, we could not touch, but his energy was sunshine after many rainy days.

Annie served lobster soup in the mansion's finest china. The smell of warm bread, freshly baked, filled the room. White and blue flowered plates encased with a gold rim served rack of lamb and mashed potatoes. Natalia kept her eyes on Ariel, and he kept his eyes on her. Eugenia sipped her soup silently while her hands trembled. She eyed everyone in disbelief. Just a month prior, her ruthless bark stressed even the birds. I swore they stopped singing the minute she came around. Now, Eugenia was silent, as if there were an invisible zipper over her mouth, guarding us from her plague. Victoria, however, sat joyfully at the table, eyeing the pink, creamy soup that was slightly fishy but silky smooth. She sucked in large spoonsful of the substance with reckless abandon. Then wiped her mouth often and licked her lips. People with that kind of appetite were usually described as plump and jolly. Victoria, however, was thin and frail.

As it turned out, someone was infusing her beverages with a light sedative, which kept Victoria anesthetized. We couldn't prove it, but everyone assumed it was Eugenia. Jackie hired local men to guard both her room and her mother's. Victoria slowly recovered.

"Margarita, lobster soup is your favorite!" Victoria pointed out. Eugenia's eyes bulged. She held her tongue. The urge to rise and smack the older woman loomed over her like a dark rain cloud ready to explode.

"Yes, Mother, Margarita loved lobster soup," Jackie whispered, taking pleasure in Eugenia's suffering. She winked at me conspicuously.

"Aunt Jackie, what's going on?" Natalia spoke. "Is there a private joke about Margarita Del Mar, no one mentioned," she asked jovially.

"Natalia, Margarita Del Mar was my best friend. Mother believes Carolina resembles her slightly and I agree."

Natalia sat back. She pressed down on her breastbone. As much as I wanted to believe Nat was a modern girl in 1934, her mannerisms sometimes reminded me she was still very much a debutant.

"How so?" she questioned. "W-h-a-t about the dead girl, l-o-o-k-s like Carolina?" she stuttered.

Jackie's brow furrowed, "Well, my dear, her facial expressions. That's all!"

The girl turned towards me, "Wow, Caro really?" She twisted uncomfortably in her chair. Was it me or that God awful corset she wore that made her uncomfortable?

I smiled nervously. My shoulders shrugged. I leaned my head over the bowl of soup, sipping closely to avoid eye contact.

Victoria smiled. She put down her napkin and grabbed her glass of water. She held it up and toasted with everyone else. "*En hora buena!*" Natalia, Carlotta, and Harry clapped. Everyone except Eugenia and Josef smiled.

"Mrs. Cervantes Alameda, do you remember Ms. Delmar, well?" Harry asked. He sat there with a grin, eyeing Eugenia. He knew this conversation irked her. Unlike me, Harry had no problem watching the woman squirm.

"Why yes, dear!" Victoria countered, turning in her chair. She sat upright and crossed her arms on her lap. She searched around the room.

"Ah, yes, the spring ball of 1895 was all the rage back in my day. April 15, 1895. Margarita was a beauty with her caramel-colored wavy hair and her deep penetrating hazel eyes that grabbed your heart. That is how my beloved Esteban described her!" she grabbed her throat and rubbed her neck momentarily. Her eyes welled up with tears, and she covered her mouth.

"Mrs. Cervantes," Harry offered his handkerchief. She took it and sobbed.

"Oh, Mother," Jackie cried.

But Victoria shook her head. "I need to let this out of my system before I die."

Jackie frowned. Her eyes darted back to me. Distraction. I shot up out of my seat and smacked my wine glass with the napkin. Red wine spilled all over the linen, spreading like wildfire. Eugenia remained unmoved. She ignored it and continued to hound the older woman for information. She persisted questioning the older woman.

"What is it, Mother? Do tell!" she said smiling.

Jackie flashed daggers in her direction. Eugenia continued the inquisition! Her drama-filled ruse to push the old woman to the brink of death was obvious. Jackie stirred in her seat. Josef rolled his eyes. He scratched his bushy beard quickly. Nervous tick, I guessed. The atmosphere grew tense. Natalia gripped Ariel's hands under the table. They stared at each other in silence. Jackie stood up and pushed her chair aside.

"Mother, that's enough for the evening!" she declared.

"No, Jackie!" Eugenia pounded her fist on the table. "She regaled us with the story of Margarita Del Mar. Let her speak before she dies!" Eugenia demanded. Jackie scoffed. Her fists balled. "Unless you're afraid, my dear?" Eugenia teased. She sucked in another gulp of her red wine then let out a laugh.

Everyone's postures stiffened except Carlotta. The short woman with dark curly hair smiled and nodded along while sipping her espresso. Her green eyes widened at the sound of each woman's declaration. Her head bopping sideways, like a person watching a game of ping-pong. Side to side! Carlotta's expression lightened with the women's ongoing banter. But Harry hadn't noticed. His eyes focused on Jackie. The look of concern on his face, coupled with Carlotta's evil expression, painted a grim picture of the couple's outlook. They were so different.

Jackie stomped her feet and walked around the table to confront Eugenia. "Afraid of what, Impostor?" Jackie shouted. She was ready to pounce.

"Ladies, ladies, please stop this!" Victoria ordered. She removed her glasses and raised her hand in the air. "I want to tell my story!"

"My dear, Natty," she stared at the wall, "Margarita Del Mar turned heads at the age of eighteen. Her delicate disposition and silky, smooth caramel-colored hair left most men smitten! As the sole heir to her parent's fortune, suitors flocked to her. Umberto Del Mar Ruiz and his wife Angela Margarita Valle-Soto her parents boasted a dowery of 100,000 pounds on her behalf. The family settled in Madrid. She met my daughter Jackie at a boarding school in London, and they became fast friends. At eighteen, her parents granted her passage to Austria accompanied by two chaperones to attend the Mansion's spring ball." Victoria beamed with pride. "The day she arrived, she wandered into the parlor where my son Esteban's portrait was drawn."

Jackie smiled at me, her eyes beaming. The memory of her brother posing in his uniform was etched in my mind, as much as in hers—the image of a man who melted my heart and filled me with passion. I remembered the day of our introduction, clearly.

"Pardon me, Mrs. Cervantes, dessert is served," Franz offered.

Vanilla custard with melted caramel, like crème brûlée but lighter in consistency. My second favorite. My thought of sweets quickly scattered, plunging me back to 1895. I was just as lost in the memory of Esteban as Victoria and Jackie were. Harry eyed me curiously. He was very observant. For one second, my eyes met his. A somber look. Concern. Pain.

"Ignore him," I told myself. Maybe it was my misgivings about his impending nuptials that lured me into thinking that way. How could Harry be sad? He was marrying the woman he loved.

Just then, Esteban's ghost appeared. He smiled at his mother and sister. A tear rolled down my cheek.

"Thank you, Maggie, for bringing Jackie back to me," I heard him say. "You must follow through and find the culprit!"

I nodded. I stared at them, unaware there were others watching me. My heart pounded. Victoria's eyes brimmed. Her wide smile and flowy hand gestures focused on party planning, invitations, and musical arrangements for the ball. For anyone watching, she exemplified happiness. The throes of dementia sequestered her thoughts most of the time. Some days, however, the imagery emerged clear as a bell.

"Caro, Caro," Natalia hollered, "wake up, Caro. Your eyes are open but you're in a trance. Are you well?" she said, yanking my sleeve.

My vision returned, adjusting the view.

"Can we get more wine, please?" Carlotta muttered. She raised her hands, yawned, and covered her mouth. She then doodled in a circular motion on the tablecloth.

"Bored, huh?" Harry asked.

"Oh, Harry," she let out a sigh and glanced at her wristwatch. "This dinner is stuffy. Can we leave soon?" She raised her hand and rested her fingers on the back of his neck. Josef glared at her and then turned his gaze towards Jackie.

She nodded. "It's their celebration."

Josef's neck strained. His veins popped as he shifted uncomfortably. He appeared put off by having to serve a servant. Carlotta was in for it! Her behavior at the table clearly upset him and Eugenia. He gritted his teeth. "Yes, ma'am!" Poor Harry, I thought.

Dinner went off without a hitch after the initial confrontation. Jackie celebrated her mother's happiness, even if short-lived. Her fear that Victoria's memories would reveal the sinister tale of Maggie's death dissipated as the night went on. Victoria's lucidity involved the parties with

THE MANSION OF CERVANTES

the special dinners attracting attention. Eugenia's face continued to sink. After a couple of hours, the mundane talk of the 1800s became too much for her. Disillusionment set in. She openly stared at us, pinching her lips with tented hands, while shaking her head.

The conversation moved to the patio where refreshments were prepared, and the tables set with white and gold linens. Carlotta and Harry invited friends and family from town while Genny and Gaspar sat and chatted with their spouses. Children ran around the patio chasing each other; the sound of laughter reverberated throughout the hallways of the mansion. The moonlight's reflection reminded me of life's preciousness. My past, the hospital, my family's abandonment all seemed pointless. The house lived again. Just like Jackie wanted. My name was Margarita Del Mar. A woman reborn into a life of luxury. Loved like no other by a man I did not know. All my sufferings as Carolina, would have dissipated in an instant, had I known this was my destiny.

CHAPTER 16

Wedding Bells

"Harrison Michael Jones, do you take this woman to be your lawfully wedded wife, to have and to hold from this day forward?" the priest asked.

"I do," Harry replied. His gaze locked with his new bride. The woman's veil covered her face. The moment of truth.

"I now pronounce you husband and wife; you may kiss the bride."

The words pained me. Harry lifted her veil and leaned in softly. Their lips locked. A warm embrace. My lips let out a soft groan. Images of Harry flooded my mind. Our four years together. My best friend. Nothing prepared me for that level of grief. I'd lost him! Sitting on that bench, watching him get married, was worse than my parents' abandonment. The knot in my throat choked my speech. To make matters worse, Carlotta looked spectacular in her white lace gown and long, white veil. Initially, her features struck me as ordinary and unimportant. But upon closer inspection, the truth was undeniable. She was a rare beauty—her bold green eyes and short black curls. The dainty tiara, with a midsized pearl that draped in the center of her forehead, adorned her heart-shaped face. Her tiny figure, voluptuous in all the right places, floored me.

"Betsy Bop!" I declared to myself. The famous cartoon character in a wedding dress. Sassy in every way. She was everything I wasn't. The big hat I'd worn sideways to cover my face didn't work well. Everyone watched me sob. My white gloves drenched from the tears. My face beet red.

"Caro, you will get through this," Natalia whispered. "This must be so hard for you."

She stood behind me in her light green dress and matching hat, rubbing my back with her hand.

"Wipe your face," she added.

Jackie handed me a napkin she extracted from her purse. The women flanked me on each side. They became my allies amid strange circumstances. My sisters, despite the age difference. They understood my pain. He deserved better than Carlotta. Sure, she loved him, but she lacked integrity. Everyone at the mansion murmured that Carlotta worked for Josef on special projects. They didn't trust her. Even so, Jackie made the evening special by planning an elaborate wedding reception on the patio for them. She did it for Harry. Besides, she planned to sell the home soon. The wedding provided a chance for everyone to relax and have a party. Now that we knew it wasn't haunted by an evil presence, our time was limited.

After the ceremony, Harry motioned me to a small table adorned with red roses and candles. Carlotta's choice—red and vibrant. He grabbed my hand and leaned in about three inches from my face.

"Chief, are you well?" he asked somberly.

"Of course, I am."

He spread his hands and hugged me warmly. His closeness lacked decorum, but I didn't care. We held each other a few minutes, crying. I pulled away, wiped my tears.

"By the way, I got you a wedding present," I offered.

He eyed me warily. "Your presence here is enough. I've disappointed you. Abandoned you to marry someone else," he muttered. "It's unforgivable, you would have never . . ."

I shook my head. "Harry, you're in love and happy! That's all I want for you; besides, we will always be family. Someday you will return to Virginia Beach."

He pulled out a flimsy chair and sat directly in front of me. He smiled and tossed a couple of grapes into his mouth. "I will always love you, Carolina!" he declared.

My heart skipped a beat. "I know. I love you too!"

I wanted to thrust myself into his arms and beg him not to leave me. The little girl in me wanted to be chosen for once.

He kissed my hand. "You look beautiful, by the way. That pale blue satin dress complements your eyes."

I recoiled. The sound of his voice made me nervous.

The dynamic changed drastically in a few months. We developed a closeness, unlike anything else in my life. He was my assistant. Then my colleague. Now, my love. I pulled away from him and rummaged through my purse.

"Here, this is for you."

Harry opened the envelope and pulled out a check. "$5,000!" he said gritting his teeth. "What is this?" His eyes widened.

"It's yours!" I shoved the envelope into his chest.

"Where did you get this?" He held my hands on his chest. My hands rebuffed him, pulling back abruptly.

"Things changed. An inheritance. More than I need."

The man's eyes stared incredulously, searching for a clue in my eyes.

"I used to predict your every move. Read your thoughts. Now, nothing! You don't trust me," he mumbled. His sweet breath was so close to me that I wanted to die.

"Harry, it isn't you I am afraid of. Please, please, keep this gesture a secret from Carlotta. Wait five years before you tell her. Promise me!"

He closed his eyes and gripped the envelope. "No, I don't deserve it," he argued. "Jackie's lawyer set it up. He has the details. This is confidential," I spoke, firmly.

"Your secrets will always be safe with me," he said, again squeezing my hand.

I wasn't sure what had gotten into him tonight. His flirtatious nature always evaded me. Tonight, it excited me. The man was married, and yet, I wanted him. Not as a colleague, an assistant, or friend. And not, as a brother!

Carlotta watched us out of the corner of her eye, eyebrows raised. Fresh lipstick readily applied. She strutted towards us.

"Hi, is everything good between you two?"

She leaned in and held her veil in a bunch on the side of her waist. No sooner had he raised his head, she grabbed his hand, and with her free hand, tickled the back of his neck.

"Yes, Carolina gave us a wedding gift. $100.00. She is extremely generous."

Her eyes widened. She shifted her stance. "Really?" She hugged him tightly and squealed, "You can buy me a special present for our honeymoon." Carlotta crouched down towards my chair with her arms far apart. She patted my shoulders, pretending to hug me. My body recoiled. My hand slid away from Harry's lap. Inconspicuously.

Maybe he had a little too much champagne tonight; but his flirtations didn't seem to bother him. It gave me butterflies. Dr. Imbroglio's treatment had allowed him to gain twenty-five pounds. His cheeks were rosy. His brown plaid suit was tailored to perfection, and his brown shoes portrayed an elegant and high-class gentleman. The light cologne Ariel gave him made him irresistible. He looked dapper. His scent alone would have lured me into the depths of the earth and allowed him to ravage me in every way. I sat with Harry and Carlotta for a few minutes more, discussing the details of her long-awaited honeymoon. My instincts to throw up were thwarted by Annie's interruption.

"Miss Carolina, someone is looking for you at the entrance. He says he knows you."

Harry raised an eyebrow, eyes narrowed. "Annie, who is it?" he asked.

"A man named Ivan!"

Harry shot up! "No! Annie, tell him she is not here!"

Carlotta placed her hand on my shoulder. "Too late!" she smirked. Her gaze set straightforward on my impending doom. Ivan pushed his way through the crowd of guests and bolted towards me like a madman. The pungent smell of alcohol filled the immediate vicinity upon his arrival.

"Well, well, Sister! Having a party, are we?" he shouted. His mouth slobbered. All hell would break loose tonight. Ivan's anger escalated when he drank a few beers. I watched him out of the corner of my eye. His body swayed side to side. His eyes glazed over—bloodshot and watery. My body stiffened.

Harry leaped out of his chair, puffed his chest, and came nose to nose with Ivan. He spoke through gritted teeth, "What are you doing here?"

Ariel stepped in between the two men, attempting to break up the fight. Gaspar sprang into action. He grabbed Ivan by the arms and yanked him away from Harry. Jackie rose from her chair and walked over. The two men surrounded me. I couldn't move. I sat at the chair, head down, motionless.

"No. No. How did he find me?" I muttered. But Ivan, burst out laughing.

"You think you're going to do something, jerk?" he jabbed at Harry's forehead. "Carolina is my sister!" he said proudly. "You have no right, interfering in our business. Besides, that little stunt you pulled on the ship broke up my marriage. I'm sure that was your bright idea. You owe me big time," he said angrily.

Jackie watched me sob. "Sir you have no business in my home. She may be your sister, but she is my guest, and you are not!" Jackie argued.

Ivan ignored her. "Listen here, toots, I don't care! Carolina leaves with me or else!"

His face tightened. He spun around and watched the guests. Eugenia sat at her chair sipping sangria while the fireworks exploded. She didn't utter a word, but her eyes widened when Ivan burst through the party. Her lips spread into a wide grin. It was obvious to anyone who saw her—she didn't care.

Ivan grabbed me by the arm and pulled me sideways forcefully. "Sister, I must speak to you privately. Then I will depart quietly," he demanded. "I'm in trouble and need your help!"

"No, Sir, you will not!" Harry scowled.

Carlotta pulled at his jacket, trying to get him away from the confrontation. "Harry, this is our wedding, not our problem," she shouted. But Harry remained unmoved.

"Yeah, listen to your little wifey there, fool. Did you tell her you and Caro slept together on the ship!" His face tightened.

"Carlotta, stay out of this!" Harry shouted.

"Harry, it's fine, I will speak with him. You can keep an eye on me," I mumbled.

"No, I won't allow it!" he growled.

"You're not her husband, Harry. Maybe you should stay out of this!" the gardener shouted. "This is an embarrassment to my daughter!"

But Harry's demeanor only escalated, matching his adversary's aggressive conduct. Jackie stepped in.

"That's enough. If you wish to speak to Carolina, you will do so in my presence," she added.

"Are you sure, Sister? You want these people to know all about your past?" he teased.

Eugenia's ears perked. She stood up and moved, dragging her cane quickly toward the action. "What is he talking about, Miss Del Valle?" she demanded. She posed with her hands on her hip as if any of that would intimidate me. Nonetheless, my putrid example of a half-brother yapped away.

"Tell her, Sis! Tell her about your stint at—you know—the crazy place!"

Harry threw the first punch. Ivan's nose splattered blood everywhere. Ariel rushed Harry, knocking him to the ground. Ivan wiped his nose with his bare hands and stumbled back a step or two, then swung at Gaspar and thrashed him across the patio. Gaspar's body slid across the dessert table. Strike. It might as well be a bowling ball knocking all the pins out. Gaspar rose to his feet covered in buttercream from head to toe.

Ivan's grip yanked my hair full force. It shocked me. It wasn't so much that he wouldn't dare, I thought—It's just that his boldness hit a new low. No matter how much I tried to pull away, he overpowered me and almost broke my neck.

"Argh, let me go!" I screamed.

"Someone, quick, call the police! He's going to kill her!" Jackie cried.

My body bent backwards into a half twist. Harry pushed Ariel aside and jumped to his feet. He punched Ivan in the ribs a couple of times until the brute finally let go. Ariel shoved Ivan into a chair. He grabbed him by the shoulders and held him in position.

"Harry, for God sake's, what are you doing?" Carlotta cried. "You're embarrassing yourself and me!" Her hands tugged at Harry's blazer to catch his attention, which failed miserably.

"Caro, answer me. Did he hurt you?" he demanded. His hand was on my face as he hovered over me. Behind him was his crazed new bride, arms flailing and pulling at him desperately.

"Yes, he hurt me. I've been hurt and abandoned my whole life, Harry!" I shouted.

Jackie placed her hand on my shoulder. "I am so sorry, Caro. We will fix this!" she said, turning towards Ivan. My words pained him.

"Sir, be gone before the police arrive!"

"Well, I want to know!" Eugenia demanded. Not only was she nosy but also incessantly demanding. "What do you mean by 'crazy place'?" she repeated.

Ivan bent over with dripping blood from his nose. A bright red puddle was beginning to form on the pavement. His arms crossed over his left ribs as he groaned loudly.

"Eugenia! Leave us! Now. We've had enough of this!" Jackie scowled. My heart shuttered.

Eugenia, relishing in my pain, was cruel. "No, Sister. If Carolina is hiding something, I need to know what that is," she declared.

Jackie glared at her. She picked up her umbrella and pointed at the exit. "There is the door, Eugenia. Get out!"

Her eyes widened. "As you wish, but make sure to pack your bags." Shock ripped through Eugenia's system. Her upper lip trembled while she tried to keep her hands steady.

"Aunt Jackie, that's a bit harsh, don't you think?" Natalia stepped forward, conflicted.

Jackie pulled in a deep breath and released it slowly. "No, my dear! Your mother has disobeyed my orders. She attempts to continue this debacle, and I will not stand for it!"

Natalia nodded. "Mother, go to your room. Now!" she demanded. As much as Natalia hated this, she knew her mother went overboard this time. Eugenia's face turned crimson red. She acquiesced. She left quickly, but Ivan's presence had disturbed her. It was only a matter of time before she discovered my past.

CHAPTER 17

Empty Promises

My brother's impromptu visit was a huge blowup. Governmental agencies issued warrants for his arrest in the better part of Europe. He was still sitting in jail downtown as far as I knew. His prior antics had defrauded several widows out of inheritances. Townspeople in Vienna quickly caught wind of his accusations. Gossip spread quickly with innuendos that the hired investigators brought to the mansion were lovers. Scandalous, indeed, for the era.

As hard as it was to admit, Harry went overboard with Ivan. But he meant well. The pair's honeymoon plans of touring Venice were quickly thwarted by the whispers. Carlotta was furious. Her father didn't hold back his criticism, saying Harry behaved like a jealous boyfriend. The Jones's residence remained a tense abode. The older man's assessment, while correct, scrutinized him harshly. His daughter's behavior felt short of a prize-winning title. She took pleasure in other people's pain. She rejoiced in watching other people's drama and often smiled while others suffered. Perhaps she didn't deserve what happened at her wedding reception, but neither did we! Barely two weeks ago, the worst night of my life happened. But I managed to take it in strides. So, should she!

Distraction presented itself in the most mundane of chores—rummaging through my old personal items in the east wing. Most of it had been loaded into vehicles and then driven to a shipping yard and packed into large containers to be sent later to Madrid, Spain.

As it turned out, Maggie's parents died without heirs. The dowery passed on to Esteban was still part of the estate. There were three plots of land, which were in Madrid, Mallorca, and Seville. In less than a month, my life would change drastically. I had been warming to the idea of seeing Mother before she died. Helping her and my sister Emma became a priority. Maybe they didn't deserve it, but life had gifted me with more than I deserved. There was no point in holding grudges.

The Mansion taught me that. Esteban showed me how to love again. My protector. My eternal flame and teacher. Without him, Harry's marriage would have killed me, for sure. Considering all we experienced together, it didn't take long for him to find another partner. The forever kind, and I thoroughly detested the idea. My expectations of loyalty met a higher standard than his. Could I seriously blame him for falling in love with someone else? The fact we'd only considered ours a professional relationship made me pause my critique. This journey, a most unexpected one, tested us. Harry had faltered. He convinced me to travel, and then so easily abandoned me when he fell in love. But hadn't I done the same to him—focused on Esteban and my love for him? The onslaught of questions bombarded my mind every minute of the day. Jackie gave me the key to the east wing and let me spend most days there. I would miss that place soon enough.

One of my favorite artifacts in the east wing was a bottle of perfume, with which Esteban had gifted me. The scent of violets. Jackie had found it in a wooden box with gold framing, pulling the lilac-colored bottle out of it.

"Le perfume imperial. Smell it," she said. "This was hers; I mean yours!" she said, smiling from ear to ear.

I held the box in my hands, twirling it around.

"Everything in this wing belongs to you," she reminded me.

My hands traced the gold trim of the emblem. The perfume was designed by Queen Victoria after losing her son in 1890. As legend would have it, a Zulu tribe speared the man to death. The queen later traveled to the location of the massacre, and an overwhelming scent of violets wafted in the air. She believed it was a sign from the spirit of her deceased son. She ordered someone to design a fragrance made from the scent of violets. The scent of "undying love," the queen declared.

I held the pink and gold box, depicting the queen's silhouette, close to my chest. I pranced around the room, humming "All of Me" by Louis Armstrong.

"Margarita," he whispered, "I can hear you!"

It was the first time he'd spoken to me. He pointed to a pile of papers. Jackie's eyes traced my gaze and followed me.

"Ha!" she cried. She crouched down and opened the lid of a multicolored carved box. Inside the lid, a light yellow, ornately flowered square was inscribed with the initials M.D.M. Circa 1892. She picked up a file from the box and beckoned to me.

"Come here. These papers outline the terms of your dower." She waved a worn stack of papers in front of me.

"My what?"

My eyes fluctuated between the file and Jackie's light blue smock. She handed me the documents, flipping the pages one by one. It was still readable.

"Antonio Del Mar doeth hereby bequeath the sum of 10,000,000 pounds on behalf of his daughter Margarita Del Mar to Esteban Antonio Cervantes Alameda heretofore commencing on this day, August 21, 1895."

Jackie continued, "He also bequeathed three plots of land to Esteban. You are his true heir; and as such, these belong to you."

It was all there. My father's wealth in another life now passed onto me in this life.

"It's been kept in an interest-bearing account all these years, and it is all yours," she added.

The thought of never working again didn't sit well with me. My career mattered to me more than ever.

"Jackie, you are incredibly generous. You don't need to do this," I countered, but she insisted.

After Jackie had arrived, the screaming episodes on the east wing ceased, proving once and for all that they were man-made. Someone manipulated us because we didn't have access to the wing. Further inspection revealed that the east wing had remained undisturbed after Margarita's passing. Whoever planned the haunting had an ulterior motive.

On a summer morning in August, right before Natalia's engagement reception, Jackie and I strolled along the edge of the river. She told me about her plan to discuss the night of my death with her mother. If Victoria knew the facts, dispelling rumors of Maggie's manner of death would be a lot easier. Jackie questioned the moving sconces I described, claiming the mansion boasted hidden hallways and trap doors. Anyone could easily move within the walls without being noticed. Indeed, it was customary for the ruling class to move in and about the mansion without being seen—an architect I knew in Virginia Beach told me about it.

"Anyone else know?" I asked.

"Sure, Eugenia and Natalia. Nat ran around in secret hideaways as a child. Sometimes, disappearing for several hours." She assumed Josef also knew about the hidden walls. He lived in the mansion for twenty years.

"Jackie, speaking of Josef? What do you know about him?"

She shook her head. "Not much. He was born in Austria to a modest family. His brother served in the military for years, but no one has ever met him."

"What is his last name?" The answer shocked me.

"Josef Muller!" she declared. I spent the rest of the morning regaling her with Gunther Muller's background. The fact that those two were connected raised more questions. Harry's instinct was correct. I wanted to run to him and tell him of the news, but Jackie stopped me.

"Here let me send a note. If it comes from you, all hell will break loose," she added.

The following day, Harry was sitting in the parlor waiting for us. Jackie welcomed him and explained the situation. He was told to keep the findings a secret. He agreed. Despite the debacle two weeks ago, we still needed him to finish the investigation. Later, he caught up with me near the veranda.

"We need to talk," he muttered. I gazed at the boats travelling down the river. He stood behind me, stroking my hair. I didn't stop him.

"What do you want?" I replied. My tone civil.

"Chief, I am so sorry for my behavior lately," he said somberly.

I crossed my arms and placed them on the banister. "What are you sorry for?"

He grabbed my shoulders and spun me around to face him. "I am so sorry for everything I put you through. Ivan's greed opened my eyes."

I stared at him. The touch of his hands gave me chills.

"Don't worry, Harry. Jackie and I have it all under control. He will not hurt me anymore," I countered.

"See, that's just it. The way he spoke to me. As if he owned you. Controlled you." He pulled my face closer to his, "I can't have that because I love you. More than anyone. The thought of leaving you to find another man was painful. Infuriating. Unbearable."

He leaned in and kissed me. Knees shaking. Shocked. His soft lips touched mine, and for a moment, all was well in the world. I kissed him back, yearning to stay in the moment forever then recalled, he was married two weeks ago.

"No." I pulled away. "This isn't right, Harry. Yes, I love you too. I have missed you more than you will ever know. But Carlotta is your wife. Figure that out before you kiss me again."

He nodded. His hands still holding onto my elbows. He turned away from me and watched the mansion.

"From the outside, this seemed like a great adventure. But now, not so much!" he pursed his lips. Our eyes locked. "Carlotta hasn't been truthful with me, and it took me a long time to figure it out."

"What do you mean?" I countered.

"She has a way of spinning stories. The way she plays with her hair and bites her lips—a coping mechanism to cover her lies. It's always troubled me. The constant catering to Josef's demands even after Jackie's arrival. As if they are in cahoots." I gasped. "When you mentioned, the pattern of activity on Monday, Wednesday and Friday evenings in the east wing, I wondered who, if anyone, was involved."

The shivers ran up my spine. My hands crossed my mouth. I didn't like where this was going, but I listened in silence.

"To prove my theory, I requested permission to invite her to dinner on a Wednesday evening. A few days later; you mentioned there was no activity that evening, while Carlotta was with me. Then, it resumed the following Friday when I returned to mansion."

"Harry," I coughed, "what are you saying?"

He pulled on the curls of his moustache. "I am not sure, but I think it's her. I planned to follow her, but Jackie arrived, and all activity ceased. Then you said I should forgive her and be happy. I gave in."

My head was spinning. We'd been duped.

"Oh, Harry, I am so sorry. I was just trying . . ."

He placed his finger on my lips. "I know what you did for me. Selfless. Now it's my turn to take care of you. I will figure this out with Carlotta." I nodded. "In the meantime, there is something I need from you," he spoke softly. "Can you speak with Jackie about renewing the talk of ghost activity. If Carlotta is involved, we need them to reenact the nightly screams."

That evening, Natalia and Ariel joined our light dinner. Grilled Chilean seabass, roasted potatoes, Spanish rice, and the wine of choice: pinot noir from France. Genny prepared a small cucumber and tomato salad to accompany the main course. It wasn't the same without Harry. His departure left me feeling depressed.

After our kiss, my heart expanded. As crazy as it sounded, I loved a ghost and a human. Past and present together at last. I discussed the issue with Esteban. He didn't seem surprised. Instead, he smiled, "I want you to be happy, Maggie. That's all I ever wanted."

It was the first time he mentioned transcending beyond the earthly plane. I didn't want that to happen. I begged him not to leave me. Esteban should have left long ago, but he stayed for me. Lost in limbo. As much as I loved him, my selfishness kept his soul from advancing to a better place. We were worlds apart. Unable to physically connect. He was visible to me, but no one else. Anyone outside of Jackie, Harry, Genny, and Gaspar would have thought I was ill. My return to the mansion as Carolina Del Valle, restored his hope in all that was right on earth. Esteban knew of my love for children, he refused to condemn me to a life without them.

The swift clanking sounds of silverware touching the plates jarred my thoughts. Victoria remained in her room. Her condition had taken a turn for the worst. Eugenia, Jackie, and I ate quietly.

"Madam? A telegram for you!" Josef muttered. Jackie was startled by sudden view of a tray topped with an envelope. Her eyes narrowed. "For me?"

The crinkle in her nose made me wonder: "What is she up to?"

Jackie grabbed the envelope. She lifted the chain of her glasses and hung them above the ridge of her nose. She straightened her glasses and read aloud:

"Dear Mrs. Cervantes, it has come to my attention that you are currently residing at the mansion. I've read Miss Del Valle's letter indicating there is evidence of a haunting in the east wing."

She paused. Eugenia's ears perked up. Her eyes were bulging out of her head. She turned to Natalia and then back to me.

"Miss Del Valle, I thought you said the east wing is not haunted?" she inquired. Her tone inquisitive but not demanding. Sort of evasive.

I coughed, "Well, Madam, I said we heard screams as part of my findings in the report. But they've since stopped."

She eyed me warily while inhaling a large chunk of sea bass, flaky and moist. The reddish sauce dripped down her chin. Hurriedly, she wiped it with a napkin.

Jackie interrupted, "May I continue?"

Eugenia and I nodded. She stabbed each potato, studying it carefully before placing it into her mouth. She chewed slowly and deliberately, all while contemplating her next move.

"The sessions ceased because of a 10:30 p.m. curfew!" Jackie raised an eyebrow. Her eyes wandered about the table, examining everyone's reactions. She returned to the letter, but this time, she scanned the contents right down to the end. She crumpled it in one hand when finished and dismissed Josef with the other. His face expressionless.

"Carolina, he wants you to finish the experiment. No curfew," she muttered.

"I need to conduct a séance in the east wing. To call the ghost back," I griped, and then I gulped the delicious wine, hoping to drown my sorrows. I placed the empty glass on the table and raised my hand. "There is something else." Eugenia licked her lips. "At our last investigation, my camera took photographs. I was wondering if maybe Josef could clarify the images for me."

He appeared petrified. He rolled his eyes. "Madam, what photographs?" he asked.

My legs leaped out of the chair. I grabbed an envelope containing the photos just recently developed. I sat down and placed an array of photos face down on the table. Annie moved the centerpiece and other ornaments out of the way for me. Poker face.

"Sir, do you recall our investigation that evening?"

He turned away from me, facing Eugenia. "No, frankly I do not!" he answered.

"You were captured near my recording device precisely at the moment that Harry, Carlotta, and I ran out of the room."

He turned his face towards me. The beads of sweat formed on his upper lip. His voice cracked, "No, you are mistaken. Let me see that." He scuffled towards me, trying to block me from showing the photos. Too late. Natalia beat him to it.

Each photograph revealed Josef fiddling with the device. A total of five. One photo captured Josef removing a small device from the recorder. Another captured his profile hiding behind the doorway. Another shot him from behind, running away from the camera.

"What is the meaning of this?" Jackie shouted. He froze. The stoic figure of a man was speechless.

"Hmm, I—I—I can't," Josef belted out a deep groan, like those of one who accepts his fate.

Eugenia piped up, "Let me see those!"

I passed them over to her side of the table. Natalia picked a few and gave them to Ariel, who wiped his hands before touching them.

"Josef, what did you do?" Eugenia demanded.

He dropped his head and slouched, now resembling those he disliked the most. He arched his neck backwards, then settled erect. His facial features betrayed his usually confident demeanor. Stealing! Tampering with evidence! Obstruction of an investigation! I couldn't stop there.

"Sir, you are related to Gunther Muller, yes?" I demanded. For once, my confidence confronting this villain had skyrocketed. I stood up from my chair, pointed at him while I paced around in circles. Cross-examination time.

"You're in cahoots with your brother, Sir! He implanted the equipment with a device that you would eventually retrieve. Isn't that the truth?" He didn't answer.

"Josef?" Eugenia called to him, but he remained silent. He scowled, his face grim, but eventually dropping it toward the ground.

"Ariel, please call the police."

Josef tried to run but Tristan and Ariel caught him before he escaped. The turn of events, while unexpected, cleared the way for solutions. Nemesis number one begone! I reckoned.

CHAPTER 18

"My Brother, My Keeper"

The following Saturday, Gaspar drove me downtown to police headquarters where they were holding Ivan. Despite his behavior at the reception, some level of remorse had set in. He sent me a letter, regretting the entire incident. He said his transfer back to London was approved, and he was running out of time to warn me. That caught my attention! The level of trust between us was broken, but irretrievably? I wasn't sure. My half-brother spent his life angry at the world. His ruthless behavior stemmed, in part, from father's rejection and mother's rebuke. His displays of control over me instilled fear, and yet, he was family even when he behaved badly.

Gaspar entered through the double doors of the precinct with me. He pushed the door with one hand and held it open with the other. Gaspar's usually jolly demeanor disappeared as we approached the officer sitting at the front desk. He spoke in German, addressing the officer formally. The man demanded to see my passport and questioned the difference in last names. Gaspar mentioned our relationship and the officer briefly inspected Ivan's letter. A few minutes later, he approved the visit.

The officer updated the visitor's log with my information. Another visitor, noted in plain view, was Eugenia Arguelles De Cervantes, August 25, 1934, at 1:05 p.m. I frowned. Gaspar, unaware of my discovery, turned to me in a huff when he felt my elbow jab him in the rib.

"Ouch," he yelped.

"Look at the log," I uttered in a strained whisper. "Did you bring her here last week?" I twisted his arm and pinched his skin in all directions. He writhed in pain.

"No! I promise you! It wasn't me!" he squealed. The officer stood up; he slapped his hand on his desk and leaned forward.

"What's going on? Is she hurting you?" he questioned. His eyes narrowed toward me.

Gaspar appeared nervous; he shook like a leaf in front of the officer, escalating the situation.

"Hmm, no she's not! We are just joking around," he smiled. He coughed briefly covering his mouth, while struggling to fix his nervous gait.

The officer sighed and said, "This way!"

We followed him closely until we reached a jail cell with white steel bars, old and rusty. You could see the paint peeling off in different spots. My brother wore a white and brown striped uniform, his pale face somber. His hair looked disheveled and apparently dirty. White clumps stuck his naturally wavy light brown hair together, making it stiff as a board. He sat on a makeshift bed near the wall with his head down. His head sunk between his hands in a fetal position. When he heard the pounding of footsteps on the checkered marble floor, his face brightened.

"Carolina. You're here!" he beamed. Gaspar glared at him.

"I want to speak to my brother alone!" I demanded. He nodded.

The officer stepped into an adjacent room with Gaspar—keeping his distance but close enough to intercede quickly, if necessary.

My brother rose from his bed and leaped towards the bars, grabbing onto them for dear life. The smell of vomit filled the vicinity. My firm stance jolted him. He stretched his hand out to meet mine, but I didn't budge.

"Sister, please!" he called to me. My serious demeanor didn't derail his efforts.

"What do you want?" I asked. He watched me curiously. He stretched his arm out through the empty space between the bars.

"Caro, I am a complete jerk!"

I crossed my arms over my chest, waiting for him to continue. "Well?"

Ivan shuddered. I wasn't used to seeing him in such a vulnerable state. Maybe, his outrageous behavior scared me half to death, preventing me from seeking a closer relationship.

He paused, "Caro, like I said, I am a jerk. The worse kind."

"Yes, I know," I replied.

"Seeing you again, brought out the worst in me. Memories of father and his refusal to acknowledge I was part of the family. His son, your brother. It messed me up, bad." I nodded. "But I don't wish you any harm. I've realized your life was as messed up as mine. Maybe worse."

I stared at him contemplating whether to believe him. For once, his belligerent rants were nonexistent. He seemed genuine when he said he regretted showing up in an inebriated state and embarrassing me.

"Jesus, Ivan. If you wanted a relationship with me all you had to do was ask," I replied.

His hands hung low, waiting for my hand to meet his. Not yet.

"I tried. At the ship remember. You were having none of it. The more you rejected me, the angrier I got."

I never considered how my responses affected him. Ivan's physical assaults broke me as a child; there was no chance to heal. Slowly, we shared our feelings over father's abandonment. We found common ground in such extraneous of circumstances. He confessed that tracking me to the mansion took months. He used the money stolen from Ginger to travel to Austria.

"Why did you want to find me so badly?" I muttered.

"Because you are the only family I have left. Mother passed away. My brothers and sisters disowned me. Emma and Lillian wanted nothing to do with me. But you were disowned as well. We were both abandoned. I didn't know your whereabouts; but when I saw you on the ship, I knew it was destiny bringing us back together!"

I stepped closer to him, extending my hands. He latched on to me. I feared this was a ruse to hurt me, but he caressed my hands.

"Caro, please forgive me. I betrayed you to the woman who lives at the mansion. She paid me enough money to hire a good lawyer. I didn't realize how badly this might hurt you. Or worse, put you in harm's way."

My hands trembled. I pulled away from him. "Why did you do that? She's an evil woman!" I shouted. The officer ran in and asked if I was well.

"Yes," I replied, "just upset with my brother."

He smiled and nodded. Gaspar interpreted for me.

Once calm, my brother explained. The woman wanted answers. She told him the story of our arrival at the mansion and all that transpired. She dubbed me a liar and said I poked fun of him. It made him angry. Ivan had revealed the private information about my stint at the hospital only to regret it afterwards.

"You don't have to forgive me, but your safety is my priority. She said she would make sure you returned to the place where you came from—the mental hospital." He shook his head. "You don't deserve that. I sent back her check. Her money is no good to me. I will figure it out," he said sobbing. "Just wanted you to know, I am truly sorry."

My tears flowed heavily that morning. His confession unleashed a slew of emotions. Eugenia hated me. Just like most people. But this time, she would not win! If she had anything to do with Esteban's murder, she would pay for it!

"Brother, don't worry about the money! I will hire the best lawyer money can buy to defend you! I am sorry it took this tragedy for us to mend fences. I will not abandon you!"

I left the jail confused and determined. Ivan victimized others because he couldn't cope with his own demons, but he was still my brother! He needed my help. Gaspar retained a Viennese attorney to handle the extradition process. He made sure Ivan was treated well.

Two days later, I returned to headquarters and found Ivan in a special room with a bed and a radio. He smelled clean with a light scent of sharp, fresh gingerroot. Ivan sported a shorter haircut; it was wet and slicked back. I lunged myself at him and hugged him tightly. He wrapped his arms around me, bending forward. His rib still fractured from Harry's punches. He flinched.

"Does it still hurt?" I asked.

"Yes. That guy punched me so hard. He must really love you!" he joked.

"Huh, that was his wedding day, Ivan. He is just a good friend!" I laughed.

He raised an eyebrow and sat down on a nearby chair. I placed my shawl on the bed and sat next to him. He grabbed my hands and kissed them.

"He was jealous of me, you know! Why did he marry the woman?" Ivan mumbled.

"It's complicated brother. I know Harry loves me. He is a good guy, promise!" I made the sign of a cross with my hands over my chest. He rolled his eyes. He leaned his head back, pushing the chair backwards with the front legs dangling in the air. His hands opened wide touched the back of his head.

"How did you manage the royal treatment for me?" he asked.

"Another time, we will discuss it," I frowned.

"The lawyer tells me they will try to work a deal once we return to London. A few years in the slammer, and I will be free to start over," he said confidently.

"Yes, but it will not be by taking advantage of lonely widows!" I remarked.

The grimaced look on his face pained me.

"I don't want to know why," I begged.

"You should! It's ugly but I will tell you the truth!" he said calmly.

My brother spent two hours revealing his past gambling incidents. He racked up a lot of debt with very bad people. He paid them off by swindling women out of their fortunes. Ginger, his last bride, killed herself a couple of months after they arrived in London. Watching my brother sob in my arms desperate for redemption scared me. Would he really change his behavior? Was this temporary because of jail? Nothing was promised, but I kept my word. They transferred him out of Vienna on the following evening. His lawyer kept me updated on the status of his cases.

CHAPTER 19

Darkness vs. Light

I returned to the mansion that evening to Jackie's frantic calls. Mrs. Victoria Alameda De Cervantes was on her death bed. Natalia waited for us at the entrance of the mansion with the devastating news.

"Caro, quick get upstairs! Aunt Jackie expects you!"

I climbed the staircase in a hurry. Before we reached the room on the north side of the mansion, Jackie rushed towards me.

"Quick, she's dying. She's hallucinating, and I heard her say something about Julian."

Jackie's face was recked with pain. Her face contorted, her eyelids droopy, swollen, and red from crying. Her lips lobsided, mouth sagging.

"Oh my god, Jackie. I am so sorry," I sighed, scrambling to reach the bed where the woman lay debilitated and greyish in color. Her eyes empty. Her limp limbs lying by her side. When I entered the room, she attempted to speak.

"Margarita, you're here to take me to the other side," she barely spoke. "I am so sorry for what we did to you. Can you forgive me?" she pleaded, "I don't want to die with this secret."

I staggered towards the bed, sat on a bench, and grabbed her hand.

"I forgive you, Mother!" I replied. Esteban flanked her on the other side. His bright light shining from the corner of the room. "Can you tell me how it happened? I don't remember!"

The woman's eyes rolled backwards; she started to shake violently.

"Quick, someone get her some water," Jackie urged.

Natalia entered the room. Her eyes filled with tears. "Let me say goodbye to her, please, Aunt Jackie." Natalia moved forward and grabbed the old lady's free hand.

"Margarita," Mrs. Cervantes continued, "Julian gave you a potion to sedate you and then he threw your body over the cliff into the water."

The woman coughed harder. Blood spewed from her mouth and splattered over my white dress. Tiny spots of blood everywhere, including on my left cheek. Jackie handed me a napkin to wipe the blood from my face. Victoria's confession made me angry, but I tried again.

"Did he chase her down the stairs like everyone says," I persisted.

The woman's veins popped out of her neck. She coughed uncontrollably.

"Give her more water, Nat," Jackie shouted.

The young woman lifted her grandmother's head lightly and forced her to sip water from a small glass.

"It's the end, Maggie!" she sobbed. She held her napkin over crimson cheeks; it was drenched in tears. The room darkened. A dark blob-like figure, like the one in my youth, slithered up and down the walls towards Victoria. It creeped closer.

"Esteban, make it stop!" I yelled.

My desperation shocked Natalia and Ariel, who were both watching the woman struggle to breathe.

"Make what stop?" Natalia shouted. She screamed at me, her arms in the air, "What's happening here? Where is dad?" Her gold satin dress reflected the light behind her. Her father covered her, like a ray of sunlight during darkness. With her eyes wide with horror, she stood up and ran over to me.

"Where is he?" She followed my gaze. "What do you see?" she demanded.

I pulled my hair and shook my head.

"Make it stop, Esteban. Don't let it take her!" I groaned.

The light shone so brightly in the corner of the room. Everyone saw it. His silhouette was in plain sight.

"Is that Dad?" she insisted.

"Yes, that's your father Nat!" Jackie affirmed.

A child's silhouette stood next to him. The little girl in her pale blue dress held Esteban's hand. They watched us.

Victoria cried, "Eli, my girl is that you?"

"They are both here, Mama," Jackie repeated.

Victoria couldn't move. She had her mouth wide open, her head tilted back, looking at the ceiling and the two bright lights in the corner. The dark blob crept closer, touching the lights and recoiling. Multiple times, the darkness tried to claim the soul of the dead. Esteban and Eli, held it back, bobbing in place but not for long. This was bigger than either of them. Changing its form. Spreading its tentacles. Going nowhere and everywhere at the same time. A maddening sight. One visible to the naked eye.

We were witnessing the battle of darkness and light over the soul of one woman!

"What is all of this fuss?" I heard Eugenia say loudly.

She stepped into the room, each thump of her cane moving closer towards the bed. Just receiving one glance from the figure hovering over the headboard at Eugenia, and it quickly darted in her direction, fully engulfing her. It wrapped its dark tentacles around Eugenia's body from head to toe. The trembling woman's eyes bulged. Victoria coughed.

"Help me," she gasped. She tried to get up, but the force plunked her back into bed. It grew larger. A dark, skeletal figure, which was half-dressed, formed in the center of the room. Levitating. Victoria's eyes peered at it in shock. "J-u-l-i-a-n, no!"

We all watched the figure fly over the room forcefully.

"Everyone, quick, say the Lord's prayer!"

Everyone bowed their heads and prayed, holding their hands together. I called on Lucy and the universe for help. A pitcher of water slammed against the wall in my direction. It missed me by an inch. Quick thuds were heard running up and down the hallway outside of Victoria's bedroom. Ariel gritted his teeth as he came into the room.

"What in God's name is happening here!" he shouted. He held onto his fiancée in a protective stance. The dark force travelled in his direction. Jackie watched in awe at her nephew's body levitating. He thrashed around attempting to break free. The black figure flew over his head and headed straight for Jackie.

"Step away, you are not my brother!" she yelled at it, pointing her rosary at it in the form of a shield.

"Somebody, help!" Natalia screamed. She kneeled in front of the bed in prayer. Her elbows on top of the bed.

The room lit up in an instant. A low rumble announced the arrival of visitors. The sound of rocks passing through a pump pulsated loudly and was accompanied by a crackle. Giant, grey, octopi descended out of nowhere. Their long tentacles moved in midair in unison, flashing multicolored beams of light. Like small flashlights, they moved up, down, left, right. Their beams poised in one direction, toward the dark figures. Eugenia struggled to break free. The sound of her whimpers drowned by the movement of the extraterrestrials. Blood dripped profusely from her nose, down to her chin, and into the dark ruffles around her neck. She gasped for air, struggling to breathe. Natalia ran towards her, trying to free her. The blob morphed into a man with a cape and flew directly towards her.

"Natalia, no!" I screamed.

The temperature dropped quickly. It lasted a few minutes. To my surprise, a trio of angels with bright wings descended over the dying woman, surrounding her bed. Victoria recovered for a few minutes.

"Maggie, Julian would have killed Esteban, so I sacrificed you," she said coughing lightly.

"Don't speak," I whispered. I gripped her hand tightly.

Her eyes closed. "You never had a chance. I p-o-i-s-o-n-e-d your tea. He carried you to the river. I didn't know you were still alive. He later confessed," she said sobbing. "We made up a story to divert the attention. The gardener helped."

I watched her breathe one last time. She was gone! Eugenia watched in horror as Victoria confessed her crime. From the left side of the room, Esteban's presence disintegrated into an encompassing light. A young man in a white robe descended over the body. His presence was overwhelming. I gasped. My heart, filled with emotion, almost exploded. My breath was short and labored. We watched the woman's soul rise a few feet in the air along with Esteban's. A stroke of lighting smashed the dark blob and shattered it into a million pieces. Releasing its grip on Eugenia, it disappeared. The room returned to its normal setting with a few lit sconces. Victoria's body lay on the bed, resting peacefully.

That evening, Jackie and I discussed the paranormal showdown openly. Everyone else refused to discuss what they witnessed in Victoria's room prior to her passing. No formal dinner was set. Jackie remarked how shockingly accurate my visions had been. She felt remorse for initially doubting me. But how could she do anything else? It frightened—no—it traumatized us all. Even I wasn't naïve enough to believe that she would trust my vision without seeing it for herself.

She hadn't realized what forces of the universe were all at play in that room—alien life forms, angels, the dark blob that expanded itself into several dangerous forms. Some of which had never existed before but were conjured up initially by Victoria and Julian's intentions. They created a fictional ghost and gave it life with their thoughts, words, and actions. Eugenia, Carlotta, and Josef escalated the situation by creating a nonhuman entity—one so dark and troubled it fought to take Victoria and Eugenia along with it. They didn't realize that their behavior compounded that which had already existed. A force majeure threatened all of us along with it. The universe is complex. There are all sorts of players, not just the ones we want to believe in, I declared. However, it is my belief, that the greatest force in the universe is God, our Creator, and with him everything is possible.

CHAPTER 20

Uninvited

Christmas Eve 1934.

Four months passed since Victoria's demise. Unexpectedly, the spectacle of her death changed us all. Eugenia, caught in a web of lies, acknowledged her days at the mansion were numbered. Most dubbed her the laughing-stock of the town. Gaspar announced the truth of the hoax. She worried about the pending secrets revealing even more about her involvement. Soon enough, others would learn the truth and oust her for good.

"Victoria should have gone to hell, where she belonged," Eugenia scoffed. "That woman was evil. She used me, knowing her son didn't care a lick about me. Imagine living through that?"

Her bitterness apparent, she lodged complaints at Natalia every night after cocktails. Her ongoing protests had all but tired even Natalia. The young woman felt torn. Death and lies, it was all too much for her.

"Mother, tell me the truth. Did you have anything to do with Father's death?" she pleaded one evening in October. "If you confess, I may forgive you eventually. But if you don't, and I confirm you did, I will not look at you again!" she threatened.

Another conversation took place a few evenings later. Again, Eugenia refused to validate her daughter's inquiry. She emphatically denied any wrongdoing. The darkness scared her but losing Natalia would surely exact her death.

Natalia and Ariel paused the wedding out of respect for her grandmother's passing. The family's tradition of grieving for months would be observed. The family wore black for a period of six months. Jackie convinced me to remain at the mansion a few days after the New Year. Her husband Andres travelled from Argentina along with Ariel's parents and younger sister. Natalia planned a small wedding at the mansion on New Year's Eve 1934.

I supposed Harry Jones and his new bride reconciled. He rarely saw me. Once Victoria clarified the hoax, he rarely visited Jackie. As much as Harry doubted Carlotta, he had no proof of her involvement in the hoax. He resigned himself to accept her version of events, and she vehemently denied any involvement.

By December, Carlotta's pregnancy was announced. She was fourteen weeks along. The news hit me very hard. Any chance of reconciliation between us went out the window with news of the pregnancy. Harry seemed resigned to his new life. He purchased a plot of land and settled into a modest home with Carlotta and their dog Francesco. A chunky beagle with long caramel-colored ears.

Jackie hesitated over Harry's invitation for dinner on Christmas Eve. Everyone missed him, yet few welcomed his wife's presence. Jackie convinced us it would not be a good Christmas without Harry Jones. Besides, she wanted to introduce him to Andres. Harry arrived with Carlotta in tow. He appeared sharp, sophisticated. The additional thirty pounds he gained over the last four months filled him in well. He was so handsome and striking that it took my breath away. Sad to say, I envied her—her perfect little belly, her bright smile. It seemed the wedding trouble was over. Most people barely remembered. Nothing could be further from the truth. In a few days the *Chaplain* awaited me. My long-awaited journey back would be traveled alone. Home sweet home.

Harry carried a bottle of red wine from the Rioja region. He handed it to Jackie and kissed our hands. Carlotta beamed. Her bright smile, as she approached and kissed me on the cheek, left me reeling. She stamped everyone's cheeks that evening with a special brand of red lipstick. Eugenia rebuffed her immediately.

The servants were invited with their immediate family members to dine in the freshly decorated ballroom. Eight tables with eight settings each formed a square in the center of the room. The centerpieces filled with red poinsettia plants and white hydrangeas flown in from Argentina for the event. Candles lit each centerpiece. The red linens, and festive lights, and the garland, which adorned the walls, had not been used in over twenty years.

Esteban and Eli returned to keep me company. Jackie, with the help of friends in Spain; restored one of the homes in Madrid and set up a small museum dedicated to the memory of her siblings and her mother. Esteban's famous portrait was returned to the living room where it hung in place for a few more days. Jackie gave me his portrait to take back to Virginia Beach with me. When she first surprised me with it in the living room, I knew it was his soul who called me there, despite the human intervention. My life has forever changed because of Esteban. I told her. He was and is my twin flame. The love of my life.

Harry Jones watched me carefully at the dinner table. His eyes settled on my neck. A large diamond necklace belonging to Maggie's mother rested there. Brilliant, multicolored, sparkling light reflected off my chest. My lips shined apple red. Suffice it to say, my appearance had changed significantly. I wore a long, red, silk-stamped dress with a scooped back and long sleeves. My hair settled in a curled, side chignon, and a thin tiara crowned my head. Teardrop diamond earrings adorned me, and the scent of Le Imperial perfume covered my body. It was an opportunity to blend the old and new lives.

Harry came close enough for a few seconds before he returned to his wife's side. He shifted uncomfortably in his chair. Mostly, he sat quietly tugging his moustache and sipping brandy. Carlotta in contrast, delighted everyone with tales of a delayed honeymoon and her excitement about the baby. My life felt completely different. I was grateful for everything, but modesty had its virtue.

Jackie had hired other servants for the special occasion. She refused to let any of the long-term employees work in the kitchen. Ariel and Natalia played a song on the Victrola and danced the night away. She twirled around in her silver dress. Eugenia sat at a separate table, watching the parade of servants indulge in the high life for one evening. She hated the idea. The disgruntled disposition portrayed by Eugenia meant little to most of the attendees. She huffed and puffed every few minutes. Then sipped wine sideways, holding her cane away from her, as if she were talking to herself.

Someone noticed a tall figure resembling Josef Muller in the garden. Gaspar, Harry, and Ariel headed outdoors. They returned a half hour later with the culprit.

CHAPTER 21

Confessions

"What in the world are you doing here?" Jackie demanded.

Josef's broomstick of a stance was getting old. The guy didn't change his tune no matter what happened.

"I came here to warn you," he spoke. The music stopped. Everyone froze.

"Everyone, please, sit down. I want to hear what Josef has to say, once and for all!" Jackie answered.

"Everyone?" Eugenia shouted. "No, this is not a circus! Party's over!" she demanded.

"Eugenia, sit down!" Jackie ordered. "We've had a lot of disturbances in the home lately. These events affect the servants, even the townspeople. I want answers!"

Josef stared at her and nodded.

"Ms. Jacqueline," he paused. "Eugenia and I planned everything that happened here. Right down to your mother's illness," he began, "I know I am facing charges for my transgressions, but I will not go down alone for what happened here."

"Go on!" she countered. Harry held Josef's hands behind him. "Harry let him go!"

The man released Josef and stepped back. Carlotta approached Harry sideways and motioned it was time to leave.

But Jackie noticed her attempt to flee and turned toward her. "Mrs. Jones, no one moves an inch!"

Carlotta froze. She threw her hands up and said, "You don't own me, I can leave if I want to. Harry let's go!"

"Mr. Jones, I think you will want to hear this!"

He stared at Carlotta. The woman tried to run past Harry, but he caught her and held her back. "Nah, you're going to stay right here, Dear!" he barked at her.

"Carlotta, since you're in such a hurry to leave, why don't you tell Mr. Jones who the woman was running down the hallways at the mansion three times per week," Josef demanded. A cold stare escaped him. The woman became agitated. She looked around at the patrons nervously.

"No! He's lying Harry!" she screamed, tears flowing.

"I thought you'd say that which is why I brought photographs. Caught in the act." Josef pulled a yellow envelope from his inside jacket pocket. He handed it to Jackie, and she gave it to Harry.

"Sir, I used your equipment to capture a photo of her running. I paid Carlotta money to keep the secret. She has been spying on you and Miss Del Valle since you arrived here. Worse, she was paid to seduce you and separate you from your partner. Divide and conquer. Eugenia's favorite line. Isn't that true, Dear?"

Eugenia stood up and dragged her cane towards Josef. She slapped him across the face. "How dare you?" she protested.

"I thought you'd say that." Josef had brought a similar recording device as the one we used and stored it in the ballroom underneath one of the tables. "Mr. Jones, would you grab the equipment underneath the table in third row."

Harry acquiesced.

"Why don't you tell Natalia who her biological father is?" he said sternly.

Natalia who was now standing with her hands around her mother's waist stepped back. Eugenia unleashed her fury on the man. She kicked and shoved, punching him in the face multiple times. She growled fiercely, "Bastard!"

Ariel pulled her away from Josef. Josef's face was beet red but looked determined. He stared forward avoiding anyone's direct gaze. He crossed his arms and intertwined his fingers forcefully. His knuckles covered in black dust. Everyone watched the drama, anticipating the worst now.

Harry shoved Carlotta into a chair. She tried desperately to wriggle out of his grip and run away. Harry held her in place. He reviewed the photos, which confirmed Josef's story.

Andres confronted Josef, "Sir, what motive do you have in disrupting our party?"

Josef eyed him directly. "Sir, I've lost everything. This was my home for twenty years. I raised my daughter with the woman I love, but she deserted me. Abandoned me to rot in jail while she kept her façade. I want to set the record straight," he explained.

Natalia rushed him. She pushed him, and he stumbled back but didn't fall.

"How dare you? My father was a good man. You have done horrible things. You are not my father!" she yelled at him. Large teardrops flowed. He tried to explain but it was useless. Natalia was furious. She groaned in pain. Her mouth tight. She bent over crossing her arms and fists over her stomach. She swayed back and forth impatiently.

"Mother!" she rushed her. Her hands grabbed her mother by her shoulders and shook her so hard the cane went flying. Eugenia tumbled towards the floor, but Gaspar and the other servants caught her in midair. "Mother! Tell me he's lying!" Natalia shouted.

"Mother!" she shouted repeatedly. Natalia was crazed. She paced around in circles nervously, grabbing and pulling her hair and waiting for a response. Eugenia never answered.

She didn't need to. The answer was obvious.

"Josef, the truth." Natalia demanded. She pointed at her mother with a fierce and repulsed look in her eyes. "Did she have anything to do with my father?"

He eyed Eugenia carefully. Then faced forward. "No, I killed him. She complained about him, but I poisoned him slowly when no one was looking."

Jackie burst out in a loud cry. "Oh no! My brother!" She cried incessantly, and she bit her fists in anger. She leaned towards the arm of a chair and vomited. Andres gritted his teeth.

"Murderer! Guards, hold him. Call the police this instant."

Eugenia rushed over to him. "No, wait. No. Josef, why did you do this?" His face looked stern, and tears rolled down his cheeks. She shook him over and over. "No, my love, I won't allow it. I am the culprit," she hollered. "I killed that smug fool. He deserved it. Just like your nasty mother. If not for Josef, God knows what would have become of me. Miserable in a loveless marriage."

She wiped his tears and kissed his cheeks. Eugenia wrapped her arms around his neck desperately. "I am so sorry, Josef; I won't let you pay for my mistakes."

She turned to the crowd and said, "I poured the elixir and killed him slowly. Take me away. My daughter will never forgive me for this anyway." Eugenia raised her voice, "And while we are at this, Harry, you're a fool. In case you haven't noticed, Carolina Del Valle is madly in love with you. I knew it from the moment you arrived. You were such an easy target. Wave a little meat in front of you and—oops! —you're gone, hook line, and sinker!"

Carlotta stood up and yelled back, "I love him. You're so wrong. We are happily married, expecting our first child."

But Eugenia waved her off. She flared her nostrils. "You are nothing but a small-time crook, who thought you could be a lady. You didn't even like the guy. Too skinny for you, remember!" She took a sip from her wine glass, then pointed at me with her finger. "There were days I felt sorry for you. Pining for a man who discarded you so easily." Harry watched dumbfounded. She pointed at him. "Tell me I am wrong?" she queried.

But Harry dropped his chin between his knuckles and looked away. Everyone stared at her in shock. Jackie let her speak without interruption.

"Frankly, my dear, you gave him too much credit. Half your salary and a title he didn't earn or deserve. Madness, if you ask me. I never liked the fool. He pranced in here tugging at his moustache as if he had it all figured out. All those nights you cried yourself to sleep over that charlatan and his prostitute!" Eugenia paused and pointed in Harry and Carlotta's direction. Her mouth seething with disgust. "Yes, she was paid a large sum to sleep with you. Mr. Know-It-All! You know nothing!" Josef stood there, nodding his head in unison.

Eugenia flashed her eyes towards me. A concerned look. "I thought you were mad. Get this, little girl! There are no secrets in the mansion." She dragged her feet closer to me. "When I noticed, you were talking to ghosts, I realized this was all too much for you. I thought Harry's affair made you crazy. Josef and I agreed to send you home. I forced Carlotta to end things with your beloved Harry. For all that helped you!" she scoffed, shaking her head. "Believe it or not, my insults were doing you a favor. My daughter Natalia is young and stupid, just like you. Men take advantage if you're not careful. I didn't want that headache on my watch."

Jackie wrapped her arms around me while I sobbed on her shoulders. Eugenia approached Jackie with a wretched smile on her face, laughing sarcastically. "You ruined everything, by keeping her here! Ugh," she groaned and spun around, watching the room. "Everything became a mess! When your brother ratted you out about the stint at the hospital, I realized we invited a psycho!" her head bobbed nervously up and down. Eugenia raised her finger to her right ear and made circles. "Crazy, crazy girl!"

Harry Jones was shocked. Carlotta tried to grab onto him, but he pulled away. The scene became surreal even for me. Eugenia's words cut deep. Part of her animosity seemed justified. We underestimated her intelligence. More inconceivable than anything, were her efforts to protect me. The transparency in which she described me left me speechless. My efforts to conceal my pain from Harry only served to deepen Eugenia's concern. Perhaps there were degrees to her evil persona. With her revelation, Harry's shame was evident. My mouth dropped. My white gloves were marked by the red lipstick. Covering my mouth seemed innate, instinctual. It did so for most of the attendees.

Harry's tears ran down his cheeks. The look on his face reflected disgust, betrayal, pain.

"Harry," I called to him, but Eugenia's words had stung him. His eyes bared the look of disgrace. He glared at his wife, his mouth lobsided. She grabbed onto his blazer pulling him down towards her. Still seated, Carlotta twisted sideways, using as much force as she could muster to hold Harry back. He yanked his blazer away from her and ran. Gaspar chased after him. Andres called security.

"Daddy, help me," Carlotta cried. Her father looked around but snuck out of the premises. Natalia sobbed uncontrollably. Ariel held her in his arms. Josef and Eugenia's displays of affection left everyone flabbergasted It became clear they were a couple all along. Eventually, Carlotta, Eugenia, and Josef were apprehended and sent to police headquarters.

Before their departure, Eugenia said, "Jacqueline, one more thing. You should reconsider your belief that Carolina is really Margarita Del Mar. Her madness has affected you profoundly. Your petulant desire to relive the golden era, has left you senile, old woman. There is no such thing as reincarnation. Even if there were, 'The Mansion of Cervantes' would be the last place on earth, to house such miracles. Get a grip on reality, before it's too late!"

No sooner had Eugenia spoken, when the police appeared and dragged the handcuffed individuals away from the scene. The guests grabbed their belongings and slowly exited the ballroom saying their goodbyes.

CHAPTER 22

Fire

Lately, any event at the mansion sparked shock and dismay. It seemed the blows kept coming. No sooner had we recovered from one revelation when a few more showed up. We tumbled down a never-ending mountain of secrets, hoping the fall wouldn't destroy us in the process. Christmas Eve turned out to be an even bigger debacle than Victoria's passing or Harry's wedding. Between the lies and betrayals, followed by the ghosts and dark entities that the mansion housed, no one prepared for a happy ending.

Eugenia and Josef were held at the jail awaiting trial. Eugenia faced the most serious charge. Murder. Natalia determined a wedding at the mansion was no longer necessary. She and Ariel were married by the town's mayor on December 28. Jackie arranged for everyone's departure from the mansion on January 2, 1935. Harry did not return to the mansion. Gaspar recounted the terrible news. Carlotta was released on bail and found him. They were trying to reconcile her father told him. We scheduled my departure to coincide with Jacqueline's and the rest of the family members, but my travel plans were delayed a week due to a small outbreak of smallpox on the *Chaplain*. I opted to rent a room downtown rather than stay at the mansion alone. The servants departed early from their duties. The mansion was sealed.

"Caro, I will miss you my dear!" Jackie squealed. We hugged affectionately. Natalia and Ariel also said their goodbyes. She would move to Argentina with her husband and seemed in high spirits, despite her mother's unfortunate outcome. Esteban and Eli accompanied me to the inn on my last evening. Gaspar drove me there.

I settled in a room, placed my luggage on the floor, and washed my face with soap. I grabbed a white, long-sleeved, cotton gown that covered my ankles. The room had a small fireplace, but I wore socks, just in case. At around midnight, someone placed a burlap sack over my head. They tied my hands with a rope behind my back and dragged me down the stairs. I screamed. They stashed me in the trunk of a car and drove for a while. It was cold in there. The sound of my teeth chattering while I lay in the dark was my compass. I was still alive. I didn't understand why this was happening.

On the way there, I heard a woman talking with an Italian accent. It sounded like Carlotta, but the sound was muffled. The car stopped abruptly. Two people dragged me into a structure kicking and screaming. They dragged me inside a room; it moved upwards. An elevator. I'm in an elevator.

"No!" I screamed. It can't be the mansion. "Carlotta! I know it's you. Let me go!" I shouted. The woman laughed. I heard them turn the key and open a door. The musty smell. No. Not the east wing! What were they doing here? How did they . . . the key! . . . they stole my key. They took the burlap sack off my head.

"Carlotta!" I shouted. "What are you doing?"

She stared at me. Her face twisted. Tears ran down her face; her red lipstick smeared all over her face. She resembled a clown. Next to her was the gardener. I stared at him. Terrified. He participated in Maggie's cover up. Now he was doing it again!

"Carlotta, I just want to go home. Why have you brought me here!" I urged her.

"Because my husband wants to follow you home. He doesn't love me; he loves you," she said, laughing sarcastically.

"Wait. No. I haven't seen Harry."

But she shook her head fiercely. "He went to find you at the Hotel. You are going to burn alive with the rest of the ghosts in this mansion." She turned away, shut the door, and locked it. Darkness filled the room. I was on the precipice of madness, crying my eyes out.

"Esteban!" I called to him. "Esteban are you here?" I demanded. No answer.

The smell of smoke seeped through the crevices underneath the door.

"Oh my god, I am going to die here," I screamed. "Help! Somebody Help Me!" I shouted.

Esteban appeared and pointed to the door. I looked over, seeing his beam of light shining on the doorway. Within a few minutes, I heard Harry's voice calling for me.

"Carolina!" he screamed, "Carolina! Are you there?"

The sounds of his steps running toward the hallway gave me a bit of hope.

"I'm here, Harry, help me!"

Harry threw himself against the door a few times but couldn't open it. I heard Gaspar's voice behind him.

"I'm coming," he coughed.

A strange sense of peace came over me. It was Esteban shining his rays of light on me. "All will be all right," he said smiling. The palms of his hand pointed towards the doorway. One. Two. Three.

Harry and Gaspar busted through the doorway. Harry's face frantic. They coughed. Smoke filled the whole room immediately. He bent down and picked me up, carrying me out of the room. As he carried me, I watched Esteban's translucent light engulf him slowly; he smiled and waved goodbye. He disappeared. I buried my head into Harry's shoulder.

He ran down the stairs carrying me while Gaspar pushed the burning beams out of the way.

"Harry!" Carlotta yelled behind us. "Harry, wait. Don't leave me. I love you!" she cried.

We got to the bottom of the stairs; Harry put me down. He shouted at Carlotta to run toward us; he would get her out of there. But she hesitated, smiling at him. She stood at the top of the stairs waving. When she started her descent, a burning beam came crashing down on her. She stumbled down the stairs engulfed in flames. Her skin melting off her face.

"No!" Harry screamed. All the beams started falling one after another around us.

"Harry, we don't have much time! Let's go!" Gaspar shouted.

Harry froze. Watching Carlotta burn with her unborn child stunned him.

"Harry, let's go!" I shouted. I pulled him away from her. She was scorched beyond recognition. She struggled to squeeze out the words, "I love you!" Then she stopped moving. Harry was frantic. Another beam fell inches from me. He looked up, his eyes crazed, and grabbed me by the arm.

Gaspar made it out first. Our entrance was blocked by the fire. In an instant, Harry and I closed our eyes, held hands, and ran through the flames. The adrenaline pumping left me numb. I felt nothing except my heart pumping blood harder than it could muster. We ran outside. Harry dropped to the ground and rolled. He was still engulfed in flames on the right side of his torso down to his ankles. Gaspar ran back. He threw a blanket over Harry to quell the flames and carried him towards the vehicle.

I stood there for a moment. Frozen in time. Watching the Mansion of Cervantes being destroyed by the flames. Out of one of the windows, I spotted Eli. She waved goodbye. Above the mansion, I spotted the number of souls previously locked in the mansion flowing up into a bright light. Hundreds of them. They were free. Nobody left to suffer. Limbo, no more! Esteban was finally at peace. My eternal flame disappeared. My heart ached. We didn't have enough time to say goodbye. An eternity wouldn't be enough for me to let him go! Wherever I went, his memory would follow me.

I watched the gardener running away from the mansion. On his way out, he called out for his only daughter.

"Carlotta, *mia ragazza.*" I struggled to walk towards the vehicle. Gaspar carried me after he dropped Harry who was left unconscious.

CHAPTER 23

Repentance

Gaspar drove us to the hospital. Harry suffered third-degree burns on half of his body. My legs were burned right up to my thighs. Also, third-degree burns. We were both kept at the hospital approximately three weeks while Jackie's lawyer arranged our transfer back to Spain. A private clinic there would tend to us until we were fully recovered.

During our time in Austria, Harry and I barely spoke. The fire was still raw in our psyches. Once we reached Spain, Harry and I met with Mr. Paladino and recounted our experience. Mr. Paladino offered a special pay to cover our expenses, but I refused. We had more than enough money with my inheritance. Things were awkward between Harry and me, though. It would take a long time for either of us to form a strong bond again. Perhaps never. One thing was clear, Harry would return to Virginia Beach alone. My life would be different going forward. I was ready to face it alone. Mother travelled to Madrid with her sister to visit me at the hospital. She offered her repentance and apologies for what she did.

If anyone else had warned me about the events in Austria, I would have said they were certifiably crazy. My heart was broken in a million pieces. Abandoned by the two men I loved the most. Surprisingly, there was a silver lining in all of this. My sisters Emma and Lillian also joined mother in her visits to the hospital. Emma, especially, apologized to me for her incredible selfishness. She often said that her karma was the worst kind of payback. She ended up in a loveless marriage with a man who abused her, just like she had abused me. My brother Ivan also sent letters from prison. He mentioned that Emma and Lillian contacted him, as well as mother. We were a broken family, but everyone made efforts to mend fences.

Jacqueline wrote a letter every month. A year after the tragedy, Natalia became pregnant with her first child. She expected a girl, who she would name Carolina. Once recovered, I moved in temporarily with my mother and my sister Emma. She had finally left her husband and moved into our home with her six children. They loved Madrid and spent summers in our Mallorca home.

After a year, I returned to Virginia Beach ready to start anew. News of my arrival spread quickly in town. I found Harry Jones sitting on my porch steps.

"Hey there, Chief, looking for an assistant?" He smiled and pulled his hat downwards.

"No, thanks. I work alone," I said smiling back.

Harry said it took him some time to adjust to the loss of his child and the way in which he treated me. The night of the fire, he briefly recounted being awakened by a strong odor of smoke while he slept at Gaspar's house. He saw the figure of a man standing in front of him with a locket and a key. He knew it belonged to me and immediately knew I was in trouble.

"Esteban did that?" I asked.

"Oh yes, he did. I'd never seen a ghost before, but that guy was very persistent," he chuckled.

"Oh, Harry, your first encounter with an actual ghost!?" A sigh of relief sputtered out of my lips.

"Anyway, I am so sorry. For everything," he spoke.

"I know! Let's get back to work, shall we?" I winked.

"Yes, Ma'am!" he saluted.

Life wasn't perfect for either of us. But we would do our best, try our best to make it work.

"One last thing," Harry ridiculed. "See this telegram? It's from Gaspar!" I shrugged.

"Let me see that!" I said, grabbing the envelope and opening it.

I read the words aloud: "Eugenia and Josef are on the run! They escaped prison a month ago!"

My heartbeat quickened. A wave of fear splashed over me. Those two were up to no good, but whatever sinister plans lay ahead, I was ready for them!

THE END

Made in the USA
Middletown, DE
04 May 2023